Eaglebait

by

Susan Coryell

Dedication

For my family for all the "write" reasons

Chapter One

Home. Wardy Spinks was home, but it was nothing to be proud of. Dishonorable discharge. Sacked. Another failure. Martin-Barrett Academy was what his mother referred to as "the last resort." Some resort. Uniforms, demerits, drills, formation, lights out. *What happens next when you're only fourteen years old and you've just been expelled from the last resort?* Wardy shut his eyes and tried to block out the scene forming in his mind. He'd been over it so many times. It was too recent—too painful and real. Besides, it was permanently programmed into his brain: the beginning of the end of his career as a cadet. Involuntarily, his thoughts slid back to that night less than a week ago.

Kiser, the corridor chief, woke him, hissing into his face. "Head meeting, Spinks. Five minutes. And *shut up.*"

Another head meeting. He might have known. There was always something crazy going on in the middle of the night. "Who's gonna get it this time?" Wardy muttered. Throwing off the covers, he stood up, quickly drawing on his olive-drab fatigues. Once the cadets had had to do exercises for two hours in the middle of the night—for failing a white-glove inspection. Dust on the bed frame. It was crazy. Now a head meeting. They'd knock some poor cadet around, just to teach him a lesson. Groping for his glasses, Wardy peered blindly at the

1

clock. Midnight. This was all Kiser's doing. A corridor chief with insomnia was a hazard to the entire dorm. Nobody ever got a full night's sleep if Kiser could help it.

Wardy glanced around the room he shared with Kiser and two other cadets. Their bunks were empty—not a good sign. He'd have to hurry. It didn't pay to be late to a head meeting. He padded barefoot down to the head, the bathroom shared by twenty cadets on his floor. *So, who's tonight's victim?* He wondered again, pushing open the bathroom door.

He didn't wonder for long. They were all waiting for him, lined up on both sides of the room—a green gauntlet dressed in fatigues. Silent, expectant, and waiting for *him*, Wardy Spinks, Dexter of the day. Turning, he tried to run, but one of his roommates grabbed him by the sleeve, slamming him flat onto the hard tile floor. For a moment, he was stunned. Bullets of pain shot through his skull. Clutching his head, sickened by the intense pain, he struggled to an upright position, grasping at air like a drunkard. They closed in on him advancing in a menacing green circle, closing, closing, ever tighter. Each took a turn. Nineteen cadets slapping him around, knocking him against the wall, kicking, pinching, pulling hair. It was a slow-motion nightmare in blurred hues of olive drab.

Thrown to his knees, he ducked his head defensively, trying to shield his face with his arms, but the cadets kept punching, pounding, pummeling. His nose dripped blood like a leaky faucet. Red dribble rolled from his chin to the floor. Fighting for breath, reeling, light-headed, he pitched forward. Spots formed before his eyes—bright points of light that got smaller and smaller until pain and darkness overtook him.

When finally he stirred, the brown wall directly in front of him was a fuzzy blur—like looking through burlap. What had roused him? Kiser again, and Benson, another of Wardy's roommates, were standing above him. "Get up, Spinks," Kiser commanded, handing Wardy his glasses. The frames had snapped just over the nose part. Somebody had taped the two halves together with white adhesive tape. "Here," Kiser rasped. His voice sounded like sandpaper. "Put them on, Spinks." Glasses in place, Wardy noticed blood spatters on the floor under the blinding glare of overhead lights in the cavernous room.

"He said get up," Benson snarled, in a threatening tone, leaning down to wipe up the bloody evidence. "Keep quiet about this. If word gets out about the head meeting, you'll be in worse trouble—if that's possible."

Shaking, Wardy got up from the hard floor. He ached all over. Sharp pain burned in some places, smoldered dully in others. In the mirror he could see bruises already forming on his blotchy cheeks and chin. He tried to splash water over his blood-caked nose, but his shaking fingers refused to cooperate. The water ran through them before he could get its coolness up to his face. He raised his head, catching Kiser's eye in the glass. "Tell me one thing, Kiser," Wardy croaked. "Why me?"

Kiser snorted derisively. "Why *not* you, Wart? You're the cause of most of our demerits so far. Our entire unit is on restriction now, thanks to *you*." When Kiser talked, he held his mouth in a sneer; the words seemed to slide out the wide side.

Benson took up the tirade. "You still can't make

your bunk up right, after a whole year. You can't do a spit-shine. We've had to throw you in the showers." He ticked off the offenses on his fingers as he spoke.

Kiser shifted his weight impatiently from left to right and back again. "We even had to use the wire brush on you once. Remember? Got you clean *that* time." The sneering mouth widened into a mocking grin. "Face it, slob, you're no cadet. You're just a little wart." He flipped off the overhead light, leaving Wardy in semidarkness. "We just wanted you to know that, Spinks."

Okay. So, I'm a misfit. Did they think I didn't know it? Did they think I messed up on purpose? They never gave me a chance. How many times did they trash my bunk while I was in class? Afraid to walk near the wrestling gym after the time they threw me down on the mat and rubbed all the skin off my face. In formation, upperclassmen knocked their class rings against my head. None of the captains or colonels ever seemed to notice—or do anything about it. Maybe they thought I deserved it. Maybe I did. Geek of the week. Wardy Spinks, misfit cadet. The Wart.

****

And now he sat with his mother in the guidance counselor's office at Evanstown High, waiting for the verdict on his future. Without thinking, Wardy fingered the still-tender bruises on his face. The pain burned afresh, perhaps renewed by the memory.

"Gifted and talented, Mrs. Spinks," the guidance counselor said.

Wardy blinked and sat up straighter. Gwen Spinks leaned forward, her brow wrinkled quizzically. She had a mobile kind of face that revealed her every emotion.

Wardy remained stoically silent, but he was all ears.

His mother spoke tentatively. "Well, we knew he was intelligent, of course, but he's never gotten good grades in school, and then there was that trouble at military academy, his last school."

"We have administered the Otis-Lennon, and there is no question about it. His score was 150. He'll have to be placed in the GT—Gifted and Talented Program if he's to attend Evanstown High. This means an accelerated curriculum—Latin, algebra, biology, advanced English, and world civilizations. School's been in session less than a month. He shouldn't have any trouble catching up."

Wardy's mother sat back, gracefully uncrossing her legs. She drew an envelope from her purse. "Would you be interested in seeing his eighth-grade report card, Miss Dawson? He spent last year at Martin-Barrett Military Academy, and he began the fall session there this year, before...he was dismissed." She held up a long, brown envelope. "Not a very impressive record, I'm afraid."

Wardy gave his mother a murderous glare.

Miss Dawson reached for the envelope, glanced over the contents, folded it, and handed it back. "Underachiever," she said tersely. "We think we'll be able to motivate Ward here at Evanstown High. We believe in the power of positive reinforcement." Her self-satisfied smile made Wardy want to puke.

"I'll be taking Ward's test scores down to Mr. Whitcomb in the science hall in a few minutes if you'd like to come. Mr. Whitcomb's our GT team leader." Miss Dawson closed the file folder and straightened it on her desk.

Catching his breath, Wardy brightened

momentarily. Science hall? Would he have a chance to get his hands on the chemistry lab? He exhaled, letting out his hopes along with his breath. Chem lab. Better stay out of there. Last time, it had only got him into trouble. Big trouble. If the head meeting was the beginning of the end, the chem lab *was* the end.

"Not today, thanks," his mother told the counselor. She rose, motioning Wardy to do likewise. "Thank you very much, Miss Dawson. I hope all will go well for my son at Evanstown High. But, in light of his past history, I…well, I'm not very optimistic, I'm afraid."

"Don't worry, Mrs. Spinks. We're well equipped to deal with all kinds of students here at E.H.S. I'm sure someone with Ward's academic potential will find an immediate niche. We'll be expecting Ward in homeroom 201 tomorrow at eight. Good-bye."

Know-it-all. Thinks she has all the answers to the problems of Ward M. Spinks, Jr. Underachiever? Gifted and talented? How many more labels can she stamp me with? How about Fragile—Handle with Care?

Wardy walked several yards behind his mother as they left the guidance office and turned down the main corridor. Sounds of murmuring voices floated from open classroom doors; now and then, a burst of laughter or sounds from a video wafted by. Depression enveloped him. Although the school bore no resemblance to Martin-Barrett, it evoked the same feeling schools always aroused in him. *What was it about schools, anyway?* There had been a time in elementary school when he'd tried hard to fit in—to do what he thought everyone expected. But nothing ever seemed to work. On the playground, he was a flop. Nobody wanted to play with a klutz. He'd always been a little too fat, a little too soft and babyish, with marshmallow white skin. In class, he had a knack for saying the wrong thing at the wrong time. People were always laughing *at* him, never *with* him. Except for Barry O'Brien, who'd moved away in the seventh grade, Wardy couldn't think of a single friend he'd ever made at school. By junior high, he'd given up. What was the use? School was a sentence you had to serve, whether you'd committed a crime or not. And now the sounds, the smells, the atmosphere encased him like a shroud. The rectangle of walls, floor, and ceiling was like an elongated coffin; it was like he was being buried alive.

They reached the row of doors leading to the outside. Wardy had to get out of the building, had to escape outside—a prisoner on the run. He quickened his steps, passed his mother, and burst through the doors, gulping in fresh air. Light-headed, on the verge of passing out, he wondered how he could come to this place and be a normal, regular high school kid if he couldn't walk down the main hall without feeling trapped.

Apparently unaware of his feelings, his mother searched in her purse for her keys. "I'll drop you at home, Wardy, before I go back to the office. Your sister's bus will get her home by three. See that you two don't fight." She unlocked the car door, and they got in. For a while, they rode in silence, his mother frowning slightly as she maneuvered the steering wheel. "Well," she said, at last, "you've certainly compiled a miserable scholastic record these past two years. It was one reason why we put you in military school—to shape you up. Knock some sense into that hard head of yours. But GT—gifted and talented. Maybe that's what you needed all these years—

a challenge or something. Miss Dawson seemed very sure of herself. But I wonder, after all the trouble you had at Martin-Barrett. Wardy, what did you think?"

"I hated it. The school, the main hall—they remind me of a gigantic coffin."

"I wish you wouldn't be so negative about everything."

"I can't help it. It's the way I feel." Wardy slumped into the seat, his arms crossed defiantly.

****

Gwen came home from work. "Let me out! Let me out of here!" Hysterical weeping and pounding noises emerged from the hall closest.

"What in heaven's name?" She pulled frantically on the closet door, trying to release the jammed lock.

"Oh, please, Mother. Hurry up! I'm *dying* in here!"

Suddenly the latch released, and the door burst open. Ten-year-old Leslie, disheveled and distraught, tears streaking her face, threw herself into her mother's arms.

"Leslie! What happened? How did you get locked in the closet?"

"It was Wardy, Mother," Leslie sobbed. "He said I was being a brat and bothering him, and to go away and leave him alone." She hiccupped loudly and began crying again.

"He locked you in the closet? Because you were bothering him?"

"Yes. Isn't it *horrible* having him home again? Can't we send him back to that military place?" She continued to cry.

"I'll have to speak to Wardy about this," her mother said, disengaging Leslie's arms from around her neck. "I told him not to fight with you. Wardy! Wardy! Come down here this instant."

Wardy stepped from his room and came to the top of the stairs. He had heard the entire dialogue. "Whaddaya want?" he mumbled. He wore a rumpled, stained shirt and cutoff jeans. His hair was uncombed, and his face appeared patchy and swollen.

"My God. You're filthy. Have you had a bath since you got home?"

"Is this what you called me for? To check on my personal hygiene? Want to smell my feet?"

"Don't be flip with me. As long as you are living in *my* house, you will conform to *my* standards of cleanliness. *And* behavior." His mother always spoke in italics. She italicized words as she spoke them, underlined them with her tone. "Now. *Why* did you lock your sister in the closet and leave her there to become hysterical?"

"I caught her in my room going through my stuff. And she called me a name."

"She is *ten* years old. Are you so—so *immature* you can't take name-calling from a ten-year-old? Your father will just have to take care of this one. It's too much for me."

Wardy kicked the stair post, shaking the whole banister. "Who cares?" he bellowed. "I hate this place anyway!" He stalked back to his room and slammed the door.

"Warthog," Leslie murmured under her breath. "Stupid wart."

Chapter Two

Wardy's dream began innocuously enough. But it soon achieved nightmare proportions. He walked in slow motion in the dark, deserted corridors of Martin-Barrett Academy. The science building. Everything smelled of pine-scented disinfectant. His shoes squeaked eerily, echoing in the empty passageway. Though the door to the chemistry lab was locked, it opened magically when he wielded a screwdriver. He peered into the rounded keyhole and maneuvered the locking mechanism until it popped free. The door creaked loudly as he opened it, forcing him to check up and down the hall before slipping into the lab. No one was in the building, he was sure of that; any noise was intensified in the catacombs of his dream-mind.

The ghostly red glow of digital display lights from the spectrophotometer illuminated the front counter. Otherwise, the laboratory was dark and still. Cautiously, deliberately, his movements exaggerated in his dream, Wardy turned on the bright light and blower under the hood, then pulled the safety glass down over his hands. Centering the Bunsen burner, he placed a tripod over it. He stole a glance over his shoulder toward the closed lab door. Nobody there. Good.

"Fuming nitric acid—100 milliliters," he whispered as he carefully measured. He could hear his own hushed voice magnified by his dream. Meticulously—oh, so meticulously—he poured the liquid into a small beaker, then placed a thermometer halfway down into the HNO. He rechecked the burner before placing the beaker over the tripod, mesmerized by the dancing, burning flame. Now for the glycerin—drop by drop. Excitement mounted. As if by magic, nitroglycerin formed on the surface. Brown-orange smoke spumed up into his face. Faster, faster, the nitroglycerin formed. The thermometer loomed large and bright before his eyes—out of proportion, as if it were the only thing in the lab. 76. 77. 78. Uh-oh! Flash point!

Clumps of smoke billowed up from the beaker, blinding him, engulfing his head in a suffocating cloud. KABOOM! There was a loud clap, like thunder. With the explosion, his eyes flew open, and Wardy sat bolt upright in the bed.

Beads of sweat stood on his forehead as he tried to calm his rapid breathing, tried to concentrate—to separate nightmare from reality. It had all happened, he knew. Not just a dream, but a replay—a replay of something over and done. Why must he dredge it all up again? Would he ever be rid of the horrid memory?

Tossing sweaty sheets aside, he touched his feet to the cold floor and made his way through the darkened room to the window. Viewing the half-illuminated lawn, he tried to clear his mind. But once started, his thoughts refused to stop, spinning off like yarn from a spool—down to the last thread.

The security officer. If only he hadn't heard the explosion, taken him to the commandant's office. It was rotten luck. All of it. Just five more minutes was all he had needed. The commandant, stern and unyielding, sat behind his big desk like a judge holding court.

Slowly, Wardy returned to his bed. He lay down wearily and shut his eyes, but the scene played on. He remembered clearly how the commandant had stared at him for a time without speaking, then flipped through a file drawer to draw out a thick folder.

"Approach the desk, Cadet Spinks." The commandant pointed to the file folder. "This file tells a disgraceful story. You have been a student at Martin-Barrett Military Academy for over a year, and there has not been a single demerit-free week in all that time. Three demerits for unmilitary-like conduct in the mess hall. Two demerits for unsightly bunk. Probation for accumulation of demerits. Improper uniform. Fighting in a dormitory room. Disregard of your personal hygiene." The sonorous voice boomed vividly in Wardy's memory. "There's more. Much more. Two AWOLs in the second semester of last year. Caught on senior corridor, brought before the Honor Court. Even your grades are borderline. And now this. In an unauthorized area after hours performing dangerous experiments in the chemistry lab. Only last week—the incident in the dormitory bathroom—you were warned you had no more chances."

"It was nitroglycerin, sir," Wardy had told him. "I figured out the proportions, so I. . ."

"So you took it upon yourself to steal into a locked laboratory after hours and indulge yourself in destructive experimentation?"

"Yes, sir. I mean no, sir. I mean, I wasn't trying to be destructive—to destroy anything. It was a perfectly controlled experiment. I used all the safety precautions. I only wanted to see if I'd calculated correctly."

The commandant was a tall, powerfully built man.

Wardy remembered how he rose from behind his desk and stood, arrow straight, his dark blue uniform all points and edges, his medals gleaming and winking in the lamplight. "Cadet Spinks, Martin-Barrett Academy can no longer sanction your behavior or your presence. You are hereby dismissed from the academy, effective this date. You will evacuate your dormitory room by 0900 hours tomorrow. Dismissed."

"But, sir…my parents…I'd like the chance to…"

"Dismissed!" The commandant's voice snapped like the file drawer he had slammed shut.

Dismissed. Kicked out. Sacked. No more chances. It's over. Turning on his side, Wardy tried to relax. He was exhausted. First, the hauntingly realistic nightmare; then, the painful memory. Perhaps he'd got it all out of his system now and could get back to sleep. He'd need his rest for the first day at Evanstown High tomorrow. Home. Wardy Spinks was home.

****

Wardy tried to smooth down his hair, but the military buzz had been too recent, too efficient. Little tufts stuck up like brown toothbrush bristles all over his head. His bruised face and squat, pudgy figure completed the picture, he thought blackly as he viewed himself in the mirror of the boys' restroom. Melting into the crowd at Evanstown High would be hard when he resembled an overweight, battered version of G.I. Joe. Better to slip into his homeroom early. That way he could get a seat, be as unobtrusive as possible—and hope the teacher wouldn't do anything to call attention to him. His heart thudded dully. He'd rather be almost anywhere than here—the dentist's office, the hospital, back at Martin-Barrett. With a despondent shrug, he pushed open the door and stepped into the hall, almost colliding with a hard, muscular figure about to enter the restroom.

"Well, well, well. Who have we here?"

Wardy stared uncomprehendingly at the leering face thrust close to his.

"Could it be Wardy Spinks? The good old Wart? Where'd the cat drag you in from?"

It was Jimmo Rogers, Wardy realized, with an unpleasant flash of memory. Jimmo Rogers, the terror of the seventh grade—the leader of the pack and Wardy's mortal enemy. A cruel practical joker, Jimmo had singled out Wardy as his favorite target back in junior high, getting the whole class to call him "the Wart." All year, wart-remover jokes had been batted around the seventh grade. And it was Jimmo who started the rumor that Wardy was in the Brownies because Wardy's mother was troop leader for Leslie's Brownie group. Eyeing Jimmo warily, Wardy tried to step back.

Jimmo grabbed Wardy's shoulder with one hand. He ran the other over Wardy's prickly scalp. "Hey! The latest in men's hairstyles. Very handsome. You just might start a new trend at EH, Wardy, my man."

"Get your hands off me!" Wardy pulled away from Jimmo's grasp.

"My, my, my. Touchy little devil, aren't you?" Jimmo swept his gaze eagerly around the deserted area, perhaps hoping to gather an audience for the show. But few people were around this early. A momentary flash of disappointment crossed Jimmo's handsome features, then he brightened. "But, hey, I'm really glad you're back in town, Wart," he said with mock pleasantness. "Things have been too, too dull at good old EH lately. You can help liven things up, eh?" He raised an eyebrow and grinned.

"Leave me alone, creep. Don't you have something better to do besides push me around?"

"So glad you're back in town," Jimmo repeated, giving Wardy a shove and moving to one of the stalls.

Great. Wonderful beginning. My first day at Evanstown High and I run into Jimmo Rogers. Why did I think it would be any different? Nothing ever changes when it comes to school. Nothing. Silently, Wardy skulked into room 201 to await the beginning of the school day.

****

The tension built gradually but perceptibly. It was like a hot, humid summer day without clouds, but the air was so static you knew a thunderstorm was coming. Two weeks. Two whole weeks since his encounter with Jimmo Rogers and nothing had happened. But there was a feeling, a rippling current of uneasiness, especially in the hallways and open spaces of the school. People he didn't know, students whispering, pointing, moving ever so slyly out of his way, dropping their eyes under half-closed lids as he passed. Yes, something was definitely up—the air was alive with it. Eventually the storm would break; in the meantime, Wardy felt as if he should be watching over his shoulder, keeping a wary eye when he rounded corners. It was making him a nervous wreck.

As the lunch bell rang, students began to drift toward the cafeteria. Wardy opened the door of his locker, then reached for his lunch bag on the top shelf. It was gone. In its place lay the remains of a dead frog from the biology lab—dissected, gutted, and stinking. He froze his hand in midair. A feeling of revulsion shook him. In the crowded hall, he spotted a likely group of boys who appeared to be watching him. "Jerks!" he said in a loud, irritated voice. "You're all jerks!" He scooped up the frog remains from the shelf with his tablet. Slimy entrails slithered down the locker sides onto the floor. "Very funny," he continued. "You guys are a million laughs." Slamming the locker door furiously, he stamped off down the hall, muttering to himself.

A clump of students around the outside door forced him to slow down. They gawked out the glass top of the door, pointing up. Wardy craned his neck to see what they were viewing. There, hanging at half-mast on the flagpole, was an oversized shopping bag. Written in huge black letters across the bag was WARTY'S LUNCH. Mr. Harris, the assistant principal, stood below as he maneuvered the strings on the pole, trying to bring the bag down. But for Wardy, it was too late. Who knew how many students had already seen his lunch flying in the breeze? "Ha, ha, ha, *ha!*" he lashed out. "What a sense of humor!" He stalked down the hall as the group tittered and whispered behind him.

Oh, God. Here we go again. This is it—what I've been dreading. Maybe if I'd started school in September with the rest, instead of late. No. They'd have still found me. Even without Jimmo Rogers. The Goat—Wardy Spinks, butt of all jokes. I should have a Kick Me sign pinned on the back of my shirts. Then they could go right for the target. Here I am, boys and girls. Kick me, kick me, kick me.

They had him pegged. The Warthog. The Toad. Little congregations of students clustered around the water fountain. Nobody spoke to him as he passed. They were observing him, though. He could feel their eyes boring into his back. Probably hatching even funnier plots to amuse themselves, relieve the boredom. He reached the student lounge without incident, but the frog guts had killed his appetite for lunch. Standing disconsolately in front of the Coke machine, undecided, he glanced at the bulletin board. Amidst the blizzard of notices pinned up, a small neatly lettered card caught Wardy's eye. Advanced Chemistry Students. Lab Assistants for Chemistry and Physics Needed. Apply to Mr. H. Guterman, Room 124.

Wardy's interest kindled. Chemistry was his first love; physics, his second. The chem lab at Martin-Barrett was the only thing that had kept him going. They'd let him take the advanced course because he was smart, let him skip the regular science courses. That the chem lab had done him in was ironic. *Who's Mr. H. Guterman?* he wondered.

Then, Wardy noticed the bright poster taped to the Coke machine. Pep Rally Today in the Gym— Lunchtime. Be There! The red lettering was eye-catching.

Pep rally. He might as well go see what it was all about. Better than standing around picking his nose. Maybe he could fade into the crowd. Hands jammed in his pockets, he slouched off in the direction of the gym. It was half full. Cheerleaders dressed in red-and-white outfits stood on the sidelines, practicing a routine in pantomime. Sitting near the end of the bleachers beside the door, Wardy could hear isolated bits of conversation among other students: "Yeah, big game tonight. The Cougars, you know, from Carlyle. They're tough."

Finally the cheerleaders were ready to face the crowd. They lined up in front of the bleachers, beaming toothpaste smiles at the audience. Eleven of them. Cute chicks, too. The kind who never gave him a second glance. Lots of guys came to rallies and games just to ogle the cheerleaders. Not him. He came to see the sports. Anybody who paid attention to him would know he wasn't the athletic type—though God knows, his father had tried. But he and his old friend Barry O'Brien had gone to all the Evanstown games when they were in elementary school—until Barry's father was transferred and he'd had to move. All the years Dad had tried to make a player out of Wardy had paid off, in a way. He was a championship spectator.

Settling on the bleachers, Wardy watched as the cheerleaders began their routine. They stood brightly at attention, waiting for their captain to give the starting signal. "Gimme an E!" she shouted. "E!" screamed the crowd in response. "Gimme an A!" the next two cheerleaders yelled. "A!" responded the boisterous crowd. "Gimme a G!" screamed the next two leaders. "G!" boomed the bleachers. "Gimme an L!" The crowd bellowed back with "L!" Then, "Gimme an E!" And "Gimme an S!" The screaming boomeranged from the stands to the rafters and back to the walls in the gym. "What have you got?" the red-and-white clad cheerleaders called out to the stands.

"EAGLES, EAGLES, EAGLES!" the stands responded enthusiastically.

The noise level increased with each cheer, until the screaming and shouting reverberated inside Wardy's skull. He felt dizzy with the ringing, popping sound. Finally, the captain raised a megaphone to her lips. "Now, fans." She shouted, "Let's end with our favorite Eagles cheer. Tonight we play the Carlyle Cougars, so let's hear it for the Eagles—with everything you've got!"

She stepped back into line and the stands rattled like freight cars as the students straightened up for the big yell. The captain paused dramatically, then shouted through the megaphone again. "What do we call the Cougars?"

"EA-GLE-BAIT. EA-GLE-BAIT. EA-GLE-BAIT!" The crowd intoned in unison. They started off softly, but got stronger with each syllable.

"What do we call Carlyle?" the cheerleaders yelled to the fans.

"EA-GLE-BAIT. EA-GLE-BAIT. EA-GLE-BAIT!" With each repetition, their voices grew deeper and more concentrated, rhythmical, chilling in its intensity.

"EA-GLE-BAIT. EA-GLE-BAIT. EA-GLE-BAIT. EA-GLE-BAIT."

Wardy shivered. His arms prickled with gooseflesh. The chant was menacing, mesmerizing.

"EA-GLE-BAIT. EA-GLE-BAIT. EA-GLE-BAIT."

It reminded Wardy of a newsreel he'd seen in seventh-grade social studies class. Crowds of Nazis chanting, "Heil Hitler! Heil Hitler! Heil Hitler!" The tone was identical.

"EA-GLE-BAIT. EA-GLE-BAIT. EA-GLE-BAIT."

The bell rang, breaking the spell. Students climbed down from the bleachers, sauntering out the gym doors and on to their classes. Wardy walked alone. He had Latin next. Concentrating on irregular verbs would be harder than ever. He couldn't shake the chill of the Eaglebait cheer. He wondered what about it had affected him so. He tried to shrug off the feeling. Rounding the corner to the language hall, he ducked into the restroom. Putting his books on the shelf above the mirror, he turned toward the stalls. Something bright red caught his eye. He glanced back toward the mirror, and then he saw it. Painted boldly in bright red letters on the cinder-block walls were the words: WARDY SPINKS IS EAGLEBAIT.

Shaking, he grabbed his books and bolted out the door.

Chapter Three

"What?" Wardy and Leslie stared at their mother incredulously. "You mean he's never coming back home?" Wardy finally managed to ask.

Gwen sat at the kitchen table, her glossy, dark head bent over a paper napkin she kept pleating and un-pleating. "It's been coming for a long time," she said slowly. "We've tried to hold things together. We've even been to a marriage counselor, but it's no use. We can't live together anymore. Your father and I are separating—a legal separation."

"But where will he live?" Wardy felt numb, as if he were asleep, watching himself and his mother and sister go through these motions in a dream. "Will he still live in Evanstown?"

"Oh, yes, of course," his mother answered. "He still has the business to operate. We'll both continue to work there. He'll stay at the Armitage Apartments over on Daleview Drive."

"Wh-when will we see him again?" Leslie asked, tears welling in her big, dark eyes.

"Don't get weepy on me," her mother commanded in a tired voice. "You'll probably see more of your father after we're separated than you did when he was living at home. Now he'll have the two of you on his appointment calendar." She laughed harshly, her eyes hard.

Slamming both palms on the table, Wardy banged

his chair. "Well. That just caps an already perfect week," he snarled. "God. Can anything else go wrong?" He shoved his chair against the table, causing the dishes to clatter violently. He stamped up the stairs toward his room, then backtracked to the upstairs hall landline phone and punched the buttons.

"Spinks Properties. May I help you?" It was Nancy, the secretary.

"Nancy, this is Wardy. Is my dad at the office? I need to talk to him."

"Just a minute. He was with a client a minute ago. Let me check." The line was silent for a moment, then he heard his father's deep voice.

"Wardy, I've told you not to bother me at the office. Now what is it?"

"Mom just told us—Leslie and me—about you and her. About the separation."

There was a silence, then a curse, just loud enough for Wardy to hear. "I told her I wanted to be there when…What did she try to do? Win you over to her side, before I have a chance to. . ."

"Then it's true, Dad? You're not coming home?" Silence again.

"Yes. It's true. It'll be better this way, though. You'll see. Surely you must have been aware of all the friction between your mother and me lately. The fights, the arguments, the yelling."

"So, now Leslie and I will see you more often? Be on your appointment book?"

"Wardy! That's enough. What has Gwen been telling you…filling your head with lies. I'm busy now with a client. We'll discuss this later." There was a click, then the line went dead.

Wardy hung up the phone and walked unhappily to his room. He locked the door and began to undress. *It wasn't just the arguments and the yelling and not getting along. It was because of me. Dad tried—tried to make an athlete out of me. Baseball. Football. Soccer. He even coached some of the teams so they'd let me play. But I never was any good. My glasses. I'm overweight. And awkward. Dad's leaving because his only son is a no-good wimp. I even got kicked out of military school.*

He turned on the water in his bathroom shower full blast, stepped into the stall, and pulled the sliding glass door shut. Shaking with sobs, he leaned against the tiled walls of the shower stall. Wrenching spasms of grief gripped his chest as he pounded his fists against the wall and cried and cried and cried.

Eyes puffy, Wardy lay on his bed and tried to remember when everything hadn't been so complicated, so hateful. Although he couldn't identify the exact moment when his life began to plummet, he knew that Barry O'Brien's moving away hadn't helped any.

Boy, wouldn't he like to see Barry again. Good old Barry—his one and only friend. Everybody loved Barry. He was the type even the girls in elementary school liked. Adults, too. And teachers. Everybody. When Barry moved to their block the summer before fourth grade, he and Wardy became best buddies—just like that. They liked all the same things—going down to the creek to catch crayfish, building a treehouse, painting pictures of galaxies vibrant with color. The stuff they'd made with Wardy's Junior Wizard Chemistry Set in the basement! Wardy smiled, remembering the weird concoctions that boiled and frothed and smelled to high heaven. Both he and Barry were going to be research scientists when they grew up.

But three years later, Barry's father had been transferred to North Carolina. Barry was gone—and when he left, he seemed to take away Wardy's only link with humanity. When Barry was around, the other kids tolerated Wardy because he was Barry's friend. It was one of the unwritten rules of childhood. No one ever called him names as long as Barry was his pal. But Barry left, and the next year Wardy drifted into more and more trouble—at home and at school. Jimmo Rogers moved in on Wardy like a barracuda on a helpless minnow. Then his parents sent him to military school.

After Barry moved, Wardy stopped trying to make friends. It was not a conscious decision; he seemed to have become socially undesirable, an outcast, destined to wander through life, through school, alone, rejected. Wardy rolled off the bed and stood in front of the full-length mirror on his closet door. His straight brown hair stood stiff, growing out of the military buzz. His pudgy, squat form reminded him of the Pillsbury doughboy. The dark-rimmed glasses still sported the white adhesive tape over the nose. *The white badge of cowardice.* It was the crowning cap on the picture of a loser. Dad and Mom—they were both reasonably attractive people. How had they spawned such an ugly lump of a kid? Was he a mutant? An aberration? A throwback to some horrible ancestral monster? And now Dad was leaving. It was too much to bear. His life was falling apart at a very fast pace, and there didn't seem to be much Wardy could do about it—any of it. *The white badge of cowardice.* It was hopeless. Tears welled in his eyes again; he'd have to go back to the shower to cry some more. It was all so hopeless.

****

He could not see his mother and sister as they talked, but he could hear the conversation from the bottom of the basement stairs.

"Mother, Wardy won't let me in Dad's workroom. He says he's got the only key and he's going to keep the room for himself."

"What workroom?"

"You know, where Dad kept his tools and junk before he cleared out. Wardy's taking it over for himself."

"I don't care if he uses the room. Why should you care, Leslie?"

"Because I want to make it into a clubhouse, with my friends. It's the perfect hideout. Please, Mother?" Wardy could picture her in front of their mother pleading with big, expressive eyes.

"Oh, leave him alone," his mother said. "It'll give him something to occupy his time. Lord knows he has no friends to go places with or invite over. I've got to leave now. Remember, your father is picking you and Wardy up at seven tonight. Bye." He heard her cross to the foyer and leave. Wardy darted inside the workroom and shut the door, listening as his sister came down the basement stairs.

"Wardy. Wardy!" she yelled. "Mom says I can have the workroom for a clubhouse. Wardy! Get your stuff out of there."

Slowly he opened the door a crack. "Shut up, Leslie. Dad said I could have this room for my laboratory. He even gave me a deadbolt to put on the door. So shut up and leave me alone." He slammed the door and threw the bolt.

"Wart, Wart, Wart!" she jeered. "I know what they call you at school. Mary Ellen's big sister told her, and Mary Ellen told me." She seemed to be waiting for him to react, but he kept silent.

"Eaglebait," she taunted. "Wardy Spinks is Eaglebait."

Friday, November 1

Dear Barry,

I know it's been a long time since I e-mailed you, but things are going from bad to worse here. I guess I'd kinda like to tell you about it. I got kicked out of MBA for making nitroglycerin in the chem lab. You'd have loved it! Quick, neat, and powerful! The commandant had a different way of seeing it, though. So here I am at good old Evanstown High—home of fighting Eagles. Only they're really a bunch of turkeys, not Eagles. They put me in this GT, Gifted/Talented, program where I have to take a lot of stupid courses like Latin and World Civ. I mean, who cares about ancient history? You know all I want to do is real experiments—chemistry and physics. But no. You got to pass biology before you can take any real science. Just a lot of frog guts and fruit flies in bio lab. It stinks—literally. And the teacher—Mr. Whitcomb—he's the team leader for the GT program. God. You wouldn't believe the stuff this guy dishes out. "You're among the elite, Ward. You've got to have the motivation to match the mentality if you're ever going to BE somebody. You've got to rise to the top with the cream of the crop." It makes me barf. If Whitcomb knew what a famous research scientist I'm going to be some day, he'd lay off. He says I've got to pass biology before they'll even consider letting me into chemistry and physics.

Then there's Latin. Have you ever heard of anything more useless? A DEAD language. I hate it. I think I'm going to flunk. I'm trying to get my guidance counselor to let me drop it. She's almost as bad as Whitcomb. "All GT students need an ancient language so they can get into the best colleges," she says. The best colleges? At this rate I'll be in ninth grade forever. The Latin teacher's an old hag who's half deaf and wears this hearing aid. Sometimes everybody in class whispers so she thinks her batteries are getting low or something, so she turns the volume up. Then they all shout and make her cringe. These creeps are the "cream of the crop"? There is a cute girl who's in my Latin and bio classes, though. Her name is Meg. Meg Reilly. She's my lab partner, since her last name starts with R and mine with S. Thank God for alphabetical order. I haven't told anybody else, but I'd sure like to get to know her. I hate everybody else at Evanstown High, though. Are there any cute girls in any of your classes?

One good thing. I'm getting set up in my basement for some experiments. My dad leased out the Shop Rite Grocery through his realty, and I talked him into giving me a defective scanner from the store. You know, the scanner they use to total up the food bills? I took it apart and completely rebuilt it—learned a lot about lasers while I worked on it. Real low power, though. Anyway, I'm working on making a bigger, more powerful laser in the workroom in the basement. Got a deadbolt lock so my snoopy sister can't get in and spy on me. Maybe I'll see you soon. I'll tell you more about my laser experiments. I'm trying to get up the nerve to apply for a position as a lab assistant at school—chem lab. I hear the teacher, Mr. Guterman, is real hard to please, and he's having trouble getting somebody good. But with my "past history," well, you know I won't have much of a chance. Oh, well. E-mail a reply if you can.

Wardy

P.S. Oh, yeah. My dad left. Split. That's how I got his workroom for my lab.

P.P.S. What do you think of this—for my official letterhead?

WARD M. SPINKS, JR., PhD

Professor of

Nuclear Physics

Chapter Four

"Wardy, Dad's here!" Leslie shouted down the stairs. "Hurry up. He's waiting in the driveway." She ran out, letting the door close with a bang.

Carefully, Wardy locked the workroom door and pocketed the key. No use encouraging Mom to snoop around while he was gone for the weekend. She'd probably try to clean the place up or something. He climbed the basement stairs, his mind still on the problem of a workable substance for fueling his laser. He had built a fairly credible optical structure, with mirrors at both ends of a hollow tube, and he'd run a lot of experiments trying to come up with the correct shapes and sizes for all the parts. But what to use for fuel? That was the problem. Carbon tetrachloride?

He reached for his coat in the foyer closet. Every other weekend with Dad wasn't so bad, actually. It got him out of the house and away from his mother. Since Dad had left, she'd become very sharp and negative, going from outspoken to moody, and pickier than ever about how she wanted things done in *her* house. His room was never clean enough, his clothes never neat enough—she was impossible to please. So he just quit trying to do the impossible. He quit trying to do anything at all. It was easier that way. The horn blew in the driveway. "Okay, okay. I'm coming," he grumbled, shutting the front door behind him.

"Hi, Wardy," his dad greeted him. "Thought we'd catch the early movie at the center and then go for pizzas. Sound all right to you?"

"Sure." *Why do we always have to go somewhere, Dad? Why can't we just hang around—talk? Are you afraid to talk to me? Mom won't listen and Dad won't talk. What are they afraid of?*

In the front seat, Dad and Leslie chattered. Wardy blocked them out. His mind was occupied with the proper substance for his laser experiments. Teflon? Maybe. He could buy a can at the hardware store, or scrape it off the kitchen pots and pans and melt it down. Inwardly, he smiled. Boy, his mother would love that. Too bad old Whitcomb was such a jerk. Wardy would have liked to use him as a resource, but Whitcomb refused to consider the possibility that Wardy knew anything about higher science. First things first—that was Whitcomb's philosophy. Dissect the frogs, mate the fruit flies, learn your ABCs.

What Wardy needed was a bona fide research scientist to consult. Somebody doing experiments in a university lab, maybe. The further he got into his experiments in the workroom, the more he realized magazines and books weren't enough. He needed expert, up-to-the-minute advice. Last year's book or last month's article wasn't much use when you were on the frontier of science. Even the Internet was sketchy on specifics. Yeah. What he needed was a college professor or a nuclear physicist or—but what was the use? Nobody like that would want to waste time on a wimp kid like himself.

Unless…He brightened. The letterhead he'd been playing around with. Why not pass himself off as a professor doing experiments? Write to some of the best labs in the country with a professional-to-professional approach. He knew he could make the letters sound adult enough, and somebody would have to take notice of a professor doing research and experiments on the fueling of lasers. Fuel was the key, according to everything he'd read. Why not try?

"…So, Wardy, what do you think?" His father caught his eye in the rearview mirror. Wardy hadn't heard a word he'd said.

"Sure. Fine." He leaned forward and rested his forearms on the front seat. "Hey, Dad. Who does your printing at the office—I mean your business cards and company stationery and stuff?"

"Quick-Print, over on Main Street. Why?"

"Uh…somebody at school is doing a…a project. Wanted me to ask you. That's all. Thanks." He sat back in the seat. "Do you think they're open on Saturday?"

"Probably. Well, here we are. I heard this was an awesome movie," Dad chuckled. "Hop out while I find a parking space."

"*Awesome*? Where does Dad get off trying to talk like a kid?" Wardy muttered to Leslie.

"From Melissa, probably. She's practically a teenager herself," Leslie said.

Wardy was nonplussed. "Melissa? Who's…you mean the lady who met us at the skating rink that time with Dad? I thought she worked in his office. You mean. . ."

Leslie nodded. "Yep. She works for Dad, but I think Dad likes her. You know, really likes her. Didn't you see the way he put his arm around her when they were skating?"

Just then their father arrived. He wore designer jeans, Wardy noticed with disapproval. Putting an arm around each of his children, he propelled them toward the theater. "Let's move it, kiddos. Don't want to miss the opening credits." He paid for the tickets, then ushered them through the door.

A pretty blonde dressed in tight slacks waved at them from behind the velvet rope. "Ward! I thought I'd missed you." She gaped at Wardy and Leslie. "These must be your cute children." She flashed them a dazzling smile.

"Wardy, Leslie," Dad put an arm around each of them again. "Meet Jennifer. She's a new client of mine."

Wardy and Leslie stole a glance at each other as the four made their way down the aisle.

Melissa, Jennifer. Is this going to happen every weekend with Dad? He's going out on dates so soon— too soon... It's disgusting.

****

With mixed feelings, Wardy listened to the ringing of the last bell. He was always glad when the school day was over—no question about that. But today was different. Today he had an appointment with Mr. Guterman. "GOO-*ter-man,*" he whispered to himself, making sure of the pronunciation. He'd finally screwed up his courage and requested a conference with the teacher in charge of assigning lab assistants. He knew he didn't have much to recommend himself. But the position for chem lab assistant was still open, so what did he have to lose? Still, his heart beat erratically and his stomach churned.

From all Wardy could glean, listening in the halls and classes, Mr. Guterman had quite a reputation. An exchange teacher from Germany, he was new to the Evanstown High faculty this year. He was supposed to be brilliant but cold when it came to teacher-student relationships. And very exacting. That would have been enough to intimidate Wardy into staying away, except that physics was the teacher's specialty. Rumor had it Mr. Guterman held several advanced degrees and was well known in his own country for his research and experimentation in physics. He'd taught in a prestigious private school in Germany. There was some gossip about a scandal involving Guterman there, but Wardy didn't know any details. This was too good a chance to be missed. Wardy couldn't rest until he tried out for the job. But now that the time had come, he was having second thoughts—in fact, he was scared to death.

His feet slowed at the door to Mr. Guterman's office. *I must be crazy to be doing this.* What would he say when the teacher asked about his experience? "Oh, I'm well qualified, Mr. G. I was kicked out of military school for my expertise in the chem lab." Oh, boy. Why was he doing this? Could anything productive possibly come of it?

The door to the office opened, so swiftly and silently that it startled Wardy. "Ward Spinks?" Wardy nodded and blinked but could not find his voice. "Come in, please. You are late."

Tripping in his nervousness, Wardy inhaled deeply and crossed the threshold into Mr. Guterman's tiny office. Though every available space was filled with books and equipment, it appeared organized and excessively neat. He eyed the teacher, trying not to stare. Tall, straight, muscular, with flaxen hair and penetrating blue eyes, Mr. Guterman inclined his head slightly, emphasizing his strong jaw and cleft chin. The man was definitely handsome, Wardy realized. His demeanor was distinctly businesslike, rigid almost.

"Now. Let us talk, Ward Spinks," Mr. Guterman said. His accent was discernible, but not pronounced. He had a tendency to come down hard on the *s* sounds, so that they hissed through his speech. "Have a seat at my desk."

Wardy sat down and cleared his throat, trying to curb the wild pulsing of his heart that threatened any speech. "Wardy. Please call me Wardy," he croaked.

Mr. Guterman's penetrating gaze struck Wardy with blinding intensity. "Wardy," he said decisively. "Wardy, please tell me why you are interested in the job of lab assistant."

The man wastes no time, Wardy thought, a sinking feeling in the pit of his stomach.

"I—I love science, Mr. Guterman," he stammered. "I've always loved it. I want to learn as much as I can so I can become a research scientist when I grow up. Like you." He wasn't sure why he'd added the last two words. They just slipped out.

Mr. Guterman tilted his head. "Is that all? Is that all you have to recommend you? Your love of science—your ambitions for the future?"

Wardy nodded. His words tumbled out in a rush. "They won't let me take chemistry until I pass biology. But I don't see why. I mean, what's biology got to do with chemistry, anyway? And I already know a lot about chemistry. Physics, too. I—I've done a thousand experiments." He stopped talking. He must sound like a fool to this learned man.

"Go on," Mr. Guterman said. It was hard to tell if he

was interested, or if he was simply being polite.

Wardy swallowed and took another deep breath. He had to make a better job of this, or he'd sink his own ship. "Experiments," he repeated. "For five years now—at least—I've been working on chemical experiments. And some involving physics."

"Where do you do your work? How?"

"At home, mostly. I have my own laboratory now, and some pretty good equipment, but I'd really like to use the school facilities." He stopped abruptly, realizing how he must sound.

"What sorts of experiments?" Mr. Guterman's unrevealing expression had not changed since the interview began.

Wardy hesitated. He was reluctant to say anything about his laser experiment. If only he could get the fuel right, he'd know he was on to something big. But if he couldn't, well, it would be just another hollow tube with mirrors. Mr. Guterman might think he was an idiot to try working on a laser. And he really wanted to use his letterhead, write to some labs. No, he wasn't ready to reveal his work yet. Even if it meant being turned down as Mr. Guterman's lab assistant. The silence was lengthening. He had to say something. "I—I'd rather not say just now. What I'm working on at the moment, I mean. I have to do a lot more research before. . ."

Mr. Guterman's stare was piercing. "I understand," he said in his clipped English. "Please. Leave your application on my desk. Make an appointment if you wish to talk further before I make a decision." From across the desk, the teacher rose to his full height. "Good-bye, Wardy."

That was it. He was being dismissed. Mr. Guterman

stood as Wardy silently left the office. Walking down the hall, he tried to evaluate the interview, but couldn't get his mind past one frustrating thought. *Failed. Failed. Failed again. There's no way Mr. Guterman would choose me to be his lab assistant. I've failed again.*

Wardy rummaged through the debris at the bottom of his locker. Somewhere he had the receipt for his order at Quick-Print. With the halls thinning out, he tried to hurry. He'd learned not to linger in deserted hallways; there was safety in numbers. Finally he found the slip of paper he was searching for, jammed it into his pocket, and slammed the locker shut. His locker partner had long since vacated—teamed up with somebody else. No doubt he was tired of the dead frogs and squashed bananas and wads of chewed bubble gum that appeared regularly inside the locker. Wardy started toward the door, then remembered his report card which was still in his English notebook. Already a week had gone by since report cards came out, and now Miss Dawson in Guidance was threatening to call home if it wasn't signed and returned by tomorrow.

Twirling the combination again, Wardy muttered under his breath in apprehension. A group of oversized guys stood in the alcove by the library. Together with Jimmo Rogers, they seemed to be watching him. The biggest was Jerome Osbourne. Everybody called him Jocko. He and Jimmo were both in Wardy's biology class. The other two had ludicrous names also—no doubt the result of their athletic prowess—but Wardy couldn't remember them exactly. Something like Blitzer and Jinx. *Those names, they sound like the Marx Brothers.* Nervously, Wardy raised the latch to his locker, reached in, and retrieved the English notebook. Slamming the locker, he tried to make a direct line for the door, without regard for the Marx Brothers. But, from behind, a beefy paw grabbed him by the shoulder and spun him around.

"What's your hurry, Wart?" It was Jocko.

"Aren't you supposed to be at...at football practice?" Wardy darted nervous glances in both directions as he talked. Nobody else was in the halls, and it made his heart thud harder.

"Nope. Got kicked off the team for unsportsmanlike conduct." Jocko flexed his biceps and punched the air a few times. "Little argument in the locker room after a game." He waved to the others in the alcove. "Come on over here. The Wart says he's lonely. Nobody likes him. He wants to make friends with you."

With exaggerated affability, the other three strolled over. "For sure, man," Jimmo drawled. "Hey, we could use you on the freshman team, Wart. For tackling dummy. Yeah." They pressed in on him threateningly, all the while talking in sugarcoated tones, until they had pushed him flush to the wall. Sprawled with his back against the lockers and his legs straddled, he felt like a frog pinned to the slab in biology lab. Wardy could feel perspiration forming on his upper lip—a sweat mustache. He flailed his arms wildly for help, realizing with increasing panic that all of the administrators were outside on bus duty this time of day.

"Well, if it isn't the Marx Brothers," Wardy tried to joke, but his voice squeaked and broke.

Jocko's smile faded. "Shut up, Wart," he commanded. With a swift motion, as if coordinated by secret signal, the four boys swooped down on Wardy, lifting him—two by the feet and two by the arms. They carried him to the custodian's closet in an alcove near the gym, jammed him into the small space, and shut the door with a click. Wondering why the closet had been unlocked, Wardy also realized that this alcove was out of range of the surveillance cameras that safeguarded the hallways. It had all happened so quickly that Wardy hadn't even struggled. He shook the doors, but they held fast. Under the door, the sliver of light coming from the hall revealed buckets and mops and cleaning supplies in the cramped space. Fury rose within him. "Come on!" he screamed, beating his fists against the door. "Let me out of here! Why don't you pick on somebody your own size? Creeps! I'll get you for this…I'll. . ." But his cries were muffled in the airtight closet, and he could hear them laughing as they walked away, enjoying their joke.

Wardy waited until it grew quiet, then fished in his pockets for his new smartphone Dad had given him, a consolation prize after he'd moved out. Forget the rule about using a cell phone while at school. Scrolling through the directory, he located a number for Evanstown High. "Hello? Is this the office at Evanstown High School? This is Wardy Spinks. I'm trapped in the closet in the gym hall. Can you send a custodian, please?" He leaned back against the wall, then gazed upward. Taped to the ceiling of the closet was an index card lettered with red marker. Even in the gloom of the closet, he could discern the message: *Warty Spinks Is Eaglebait,* it read.

His phone beeped. He read the text, then swallowed. *Check* Facebook, *Wart. You're real popular.*

****

"Wardy, this is absolutely *unthinkable.*" Gwen held the offending report card at arm's length, as though distance might improve it. "Straight D's. Every subject.

Even gym." She dropped the report card on the desk in front of her. "I don't want to sign it, put my name on such an *odious* document."

Wardy went on the defensive. He had known his grades were going to be awful, but even he had been surprised he'd scored so low in all his subjects. "They must grade harder if you're in GT classes," he said.

"What am I going to do with you? I can't place you on restriction. You never go out anyway. And certainly nobody ever comes in to see *you*." She began tossing pens and pencils around on her desk, shoving scraps and notes into pigeonholes, and scrabbling through loose papers. "Shall I send you to…to military school? Oh, no—I forgot. We've tried that already." She swept a stack of papers off the edge of the desk, and they went flying everywhere. For a moment, she squeezed her eyes shut, struggling with her anger. Her voice was quieter when she spoke again. "Doesn't anything have meaning for you? Is there anything productive you can manage to do with that high IQ of yours?" She buried her head in her hands.

"It's not just me. It's the school. They all hate me. The teachers think I'm wasting their time, and the kids play rotten jokes on me. Somebody just set up a page on Facebook. For people to post their lousy opinions of me. They call me…they call me Eaglebait. At school Eaglebait stands for everybody's enemy."

"Wardy! I don't want to hear any more of it. We went through all this in seventh grade. Remember? No more. I can't stand it. I've got enough problems of my own trying to raise two children without a father, keeping food on the table, managing a career. I can't be worrying about somebody else's problems, too." Snatching the report card, she scribbled her name on the back. "Here. If you fail, you fail. I have officially given up." She stalked out of the room.

Officially? You gave up on me a long time ago, Mom. And I'm not just somebody else with problems— I'm your son. Doesn't that mean anything to you?

Slowly, he walked down the stairs to his workroom. He placed his books on the table, then removed a cardboard box from the paper bag. Lifting the box, he scrutinized the contents. A satisfied smile broke across his face.

WARD M. SPINKS, JR., PhD
Professor of
Nuclear Physics

It certainly appeared authentic. Quick-Print had done a professional job for him. Fifty copies of his own letterhead stationery. Now all he had to do was use it.

Chapter Five

"Wardy can't catch me! Wardy can't catch me!" Leslie taunted in a singsong voice, holding both hands behind her.

"Why would I want to catch a brat like you?" Wardy asked, never lifting his eyes from his magazine.

"Maybe I've got something you'd be interested in," she sneered, still hiding the paper from Wardy. "Something you wouldn't want anybody else to see."

Wardy lunged for her, but she jerked away, just out of reach. "What've you got, Leslie?" he demanded. "Give it!"

"Wardy can't catch me. Wardy can't catch me!" she repeated, darting through the door to the adjoining room.

He leapt from his chair and chased after her. He could see a rectangular piece of white paper in her right hand, still behind her back.

Leslie's been snooping in my room again. That looks like my Quick-Print receipt! I've got to get it back—don't want anybody else to get hold of it. He lunged again, almost reaching her, but she was too quick. Dashing through the kitchen, she hurled herself down the basement stairs with Wardy in quick pursuit.

"Ha, ha! Wouldn't everybody like to see what I've got!" she jeered as she darted through the basement toward the patio door. She would have escaped, but at the last minute, she tripped on the bootjack beside the door and fell to her knees on the concrete floor. "Ouch! Ow!" she cried out. Getting up, she reached for the door.

Wardy took advantage of the moment. With an oversized stride, he reached her and tried to grab the paper, but she wrenched away. Grasping her upper arms, he squeezed with all his strength until she dropped the paper, crying in angry pain. "Ouch! Wardy, stop!"

Wardy stooped to retrieve the paper while Leslie stood rubbing her arms, crying loudly. "That hurt, you…you wart. Wait 'til I tell Mother." Big red welts rose on her arms where he had grabbed her, and tears streamed down her cheeks.

"Well, you started it," he snarled. He glanced at the piece of paper. It was only his report card, which was the same size and color as the Quick-Print receipt. Uh-oh. Now he was in trouble. Little brat. She had done it on purpose to get him in trouble. How was he going to explain this?

There was a noise at the top of the stairs. Wardy flinched.

"Wardy? Leslie? What's going on down there?" It was his mother. What a time for her to come home.

Leslie howled with increased volume. "Wardy grabbed me, Mother. He made huge red marks on my arms." Running upstairs to her mother, Leslie held her arms outstretched piteously. Reluctantly, Wardy followed her.

"Wardy! What is the meaning of this?" His mother's expressive eyebrows funneled together in rage. Her dark eyes blazed fire. Reaching out and drawing Leslie to her, she stroked her bruised arms. In a fury, she glared at Wardy. "I am waiting for your explanation, sir. It had better be *good.*"

Shuffling the report card back and forth between his hands, he spoke lamely. "She had my report card…was running away from me with it. I had to grab her to get in back. That's all."

"That's all? That's all?" His mother's furious expression deepened. "For that you bruised this child? This baby?" Again she stroked Leslie's arms. "It's sick. Uncalled for. Violence is never an answer, but it seems to be your reaction to any situation." Tearfully, Leslie watched.

"This is the last straw. I told your father something was going to have to be done to tame this violent streak of yours. I am simply *not* capable of handling it anymore. Let *him* try. It's *his* turn."

"You mean—you mean you want me to go live with Dad?" Wardy was incredulous.

"That is exactly what I mean. It's the only answer. Go pack your things. I want you out of this house by tonight."

Wardy glared at Leslie with hatred. "I hope you're happy," he growled.

Kicked out of military school. Kicked out of my own house. That brat Leslie. What about my laser? My experiments? My lab? No place to work at Dad's apartment. Kicked out, out, out.

Slowly, he walked up the steps to his room. He had to pack.

****

He shifted the suitcase to his left hand and trudged on, holding his right thumb out at the oncoming motorists. Twilight was quickly turning into night. He needed a good hitch before it got too dark. If only Grandma Lou were home in her beach house instead of

43

away at the art exhibition. But she wouldn't be back until Thanksgiving. He could have hopped on a bus and gone to stay with Grandma Lou. She'd take him in, he knew. Instead, he decided to go to North Carolina to find Barry. It was a wild shot, but better than having to live with his father.

So, Barry hasn't answered my e-mail. Maybe he's too busy. Got to get to Barry. Maybe I can live there with him and his family. We can work on a laser—a new laser—together. In Fayetteville. It'll be like before.

A dusty pickup truck rattled to the shoulder and wheezed to a stop. Gripping his suitcase tightly, Wardy sprinted for the door. A grim chill riffled the air, but it was warm inside the cab of the truck.

"Where're y' headed, kid?" The driver's reddish beard curled around his chin, and his middle-aged face was leathery. His skin wrinkled in feather strokes around his sharp, light blue eyes.

"Fayetteville," Wardy said as politely as he could. This ride was a lifesaver. Fifteen minutes more and it would be completely dark.

"North Carolina, eh?" The driver studied him. He still hadn't left the shoulder, causing Wardy to fidget nervously.

"Yes, Fayetteville, North Carolina. Going to visit an old friend."

"How old are you, kid? Your folks know about this little visit?"

"Fourteen, sir. Be fifteen this spring." Wardy cleared his throat and strove for an honest tone. "My parents are meeting me there—in Fayetteville. At my friend's house. His whole family is friends with my family." He leaned back against the seat, feeling he'd sounded genuine enough.

Checking over his shoulder, the driver pulled out onto the highway. "Mmm" was all he uttered. Then, "Slim's my name. Headed for Lumberton—'bout an hour outside Fayetteville. I guess. Get there late tonight." Slim's voice sounded gravelly with a western nasality. He reached for the microphone to a CB radio attached to the dashboard.

Wardy was surprised to see truckers still used the old mode of communication. Didn't CB radios go out with the dinosaurs?

"Breaker, breaker," Slim drawled with an escalating twang. "This here's Slim-Pickins, come on back." Someone answered with a crackling screech, and Slim continued. "Seen any smokies out Highway 29? Come on back." He listened to another incomprehensible response, then, satisfied that the highway was clear of policemen, he sped up and moved into the left lane. "Gotta get this baby movin' if we're gonna make it on schedule."

For a long time they rode in silence, broken only intermittently by the CB radio. Wardy dozed fitfully, his head resting uncomfortably against the bumping, jolting seat. Awakening abruptly, he sat up. In the deserted parking lot of what appeared to be a suburban shopping mall, the truck had stopped.

"Time for a coffee break, kid. We're in Raleigh—take about another hour before we get to Fayetteville." They walked toward the only lighted storefront in the mall, a doughnut shop. Inside, Leatherette bar stools nestled under the Formica counter. The dark red fake-brick floor was speckled with little curls of straw paper and white crumbs that had not been swept up. Slim appeared to be familiar with the shop, striking up a conversation of sorts with a tired-eyed waitress whose name tag read *Selma*. Every now and then she darted a tentative glance at Wardy, as though she wanted to talk to him. All he wanted was food. As he ate a jelly doughnut and gulped down milk, Wardy realized how hungry he was. He'd left before dinner and had stood on the shoulder of the road a long time before Slim came along. The doughnut tasted good.

"Better visit the john before we get back on the road," Slim told him, lifting his leg over the stool in a dismount. He swaggered toward the back of the shop, then turned to call over his shoulder to Wardy. "Keep my girlfriend Selma busy while I'm gone, kid. She likes to talk to handsome young fellas like you."

Wardy ate another doughnut, observing the place without much interest. No one else was in the shop; it was very quiet. Selma didn't seem to have anything to say. After what felt like an awfully long bathroom break for Slim, he asked her for the time. "After midnight." She blinked as if frightened. "Slim's been gone too long," she said tersely. "Damn, he's done it again."

The reflection of headlights gleamed in the front window of the doughnut shop. Jumping off the bar stool, Wardy ran to the front door just as the taillights of Slim's truck snaked out of the parking lot.

"What?" Slim was leaving. Wardy wrenched open the door, yelling, "Hey, wait! Slim!" But the truck quickly disappeared, its taillights absorbed by the thick gloom of the dark, deserted parking lot. In a daze, Wardy turned back into the doughnut shop.

"Oh, I shoulda warned you," Selma said unhappily, shaking her head. "That's Slim's favorite trick. Pulls it at least once a month, I guess. I never know when he's gonna skip out."

"But my suitcase. He took it in the truck. And he left me to pay both bills," Wardy said, still dazed. He couldn't believe Slim had dumped him like that—just for meanness.

"Hope you got the money to pay up, 'cuz if y' don't, I'll have to call the cops." She shook her head again and frowned. "The manager will fire me otherwise."

Wardy dug down into his pockets and produced a ten dollar bill. It was all he had except for some change. Everything else was in the suitcase in Slim's truck. "Now what am I going to do?" He was talking to himself as much as to Selma.

"Got anybody you know to come and get you?"

"No. Nobody. Not this late, anyhow."

"Guess you'll have to do the same thing the rest of Slim's pigeons do, then," Selma said. "There's a park about a half mile from here. It's got a few of them covered pavilions, y' know? Picnic tables under a roof. It ain't very warm, but it'll keep you dry if it rains."

Wardy shook his head in disbelief. Slim had sure put one over on him—left him in a real jam. No money. No suitcase. No place to stay.

"Could you give me directions to this park?"

"Turn left out of the main entrance here." She pointed. "Then walk straight until you see the sign. Twin Oaks Park. It's on the right. Y' can't miss it. You might find your suitcase along the shoulder of the road. Slim usually dumps 'm after he's got all the valuables."

"Thanks." Numbly, he opened the door and ducked his head against the chill night air. *What a dope I am. Stranded. Abandoned. Okay, Twin Oaks Park. Here comes another pigeon—another pigeon for the park.*

Wardy was confused. He stared up at the underside of a picnic table, trying to figure out where he was. Then he remembered. When he flexed his shoulders, sharp pains shot through his whole body. Sleeping on hard, damp concrete with only his suitcase for a pillow had knotted every muscle he owned. Selma had been right about Slim chucking his suitcase, but there had been no valuables to steal—just a little money. Everything else was still there. Awkwardly, he rolled out from under the wooden table and straightened up. A cold, dreary drizzle dripped from the gray sky, making it impossible to tell the time. As he left the park, he passed several bums, sleeping as he had, under the covered tables. Holding his breath and treading softly, he skirted them cautiously. Getting mugged was something he meant to avoid. Wearily, he walked back to the shopping mall, which was completely deserted. Not a car or person anywhere. Wardy pulled out his cell phone and scrolled down to Barry's number—a landline. It was all he had stored in his directory.

The phone rang five times. Six. "Hello?" It was Barry's voice.

Thank goodness. "Barry! It's Wardy. Wardy Spinks. I'm in North Carolina."

"Wardy? It's six o'clock in the morning. You woke me up."

"Sorry. I'm kinda in trouble. I need help bad. Stranded in a shopping mall outside Raleigh. . ." He peered out at the sign. "The Jamesway Mall."

"What d'y want me to do?" Barry sounded sleepy.

"Do you think your brother could drive you down here to get me? I've run away from home. Hitch-hiked."

He listened to a long silence.

"Okay. I'll see if I can get Rob to do it. But it'll take us over an hour to get there. Don't leave, okay?"

Wardy heaved a sigh of relief. "Thanks, Barry. You're saving my life."

"It's okay. Geez. It's a good thing I got to the phone before it woke up my mom. She'd have a hissy fit."

Wardy gave a weary sigh as he lowered himself to the curb. He'd been lucky to connect with Barry, and he knew it. Maybe things would start to change for the better. Maybe his luck was improving.

Chapter Six

At first Wardy didn't notice the police car cruising the mall parking lot. Moving in slow circles, it finally caught his eye. Evidently, the police were there for a reason, searching for something—or someone. Him? That wasn't possible. Except for Barry, nobody knew his whereabouts. But the cops were definitely patrolling the area. The driver, a uniformed officer, turned his head to peer out the window at the storefronts. His companion rested a bullhorn on the opened window of the car, as if ready at a moment's notice to broadcast some vital message.

"Freeze, kid!" Startled, Wardy did just that. The policeman's voice, magnified through the bullhorn, boomed across the wet morning air in the deserted mall. With a lurch, the patrol car stopped in front of Wardy. The two officers jumped out, not bothering to close the doors, and advanced rapidly toward him. Wardy darted to the left, but one officer grabbed his shoulders and spun him to face the patrol car. The other clamped handcuffs to his wrists.

"You're not going anywhere," the first policeman said.

"Ward Spinks, Jr.?" the second queried. "Are you Ward Spinks, Jr.?"

"Yeah. But how…?"

"Shut up and follow me," the first cop said.

Roughly, he shoved Wardy into the backseat, tossing his suitcase in after him. Then both men climbed into the front and slammed the doors.

It was a short ride back to the police station where they took him, still handcuffed, into a nearly empty room with a desk, a table, and a couple of chairs—nothing else except bare white walls. Not even a window. The room reeked of cigarette smoke. A policeman motioned toward one of the chairs at the table. "Wait here," he ordered. "Someone will be in soon." Alone in the room for what seemed an interminable amount of time, Wardy waited, wondering what would happen. He wished they'd taken off the handcuffs, which bit into his wrists like sharp teeth. Finally, the door opened, and a sallow-faced man in a rumpled brown suit came in and sat down across from him. He carried a clipboard and pen. For a moment he glared at Wardy, then he tapped the clipboard with the pen.

"Another lousy runaway," he said. "What's the matter with you snot-nosed kids, anyways? Your mommies and daddies spend years spoiling you, and then they come running to us to help out when their little darlings decide to take a hike." His glare intensified.

"You mean…" Wardy began, but the man cut him off.

"Shut up, punk. I've been up all night dealing with juvenile delinquents just like you. I'm in no mood to prolong this. We got a call to apprehend another runaway. That's all I know, and all you need to know." He made some marks on the clipboard, ripped off the top sheet, and stood up. "We're putting you in juvenile detention until somebody comes to release you officially. Pay attention to the scenery while you're here,

kid. See if it's the kind of life you're interested in living."
Abruptly, he stomped out, shutting the door firmly
behind him.

An hour later Wardy perched nervously on the edge
of a rock-hard bunk. They'd taken all his "personal
effects"—his cell phone, even his comb—searched him
thoroughly, and thrown him into a shower. Then they'd
made him dress in detention garb—denim pants and
shirt—and ushered him into a "living unit" that
contained eleven rooms centered around a lounge area
with a TV, ping-pong table, and couches. "His" room
contained a built-in bed, a window, and a door that
locked from the outside. Ten other boys mingled in the
lounge area, but Wardy made no move to join them.
Walking past them to his room had been enough contact.
They all appeared to be rough-tough guys exuding
hostility with every gesture—and their hard-eyed stares
told Wardy that they had already sized him up for
Eaglebait. No. He'd just wait, sitting on the edge of the
bed. Wait and see if somebody would come to bail him
out.

An eternity later, a guard appeared at his door. He
tossed Wardy's clothes on the bunk. "Get dressed," he
ordered. "I'll wait outside." Wardy hurried to comply,
and when he opened the door, found the guard waiting
as promised. "Follow me," he barked.

They entered a reception room. White-faced and
red-eyed, his mother sat in a plastic chair pushed against
the wall, drooping limp as a rag doll. She barely glanced
at him.

A guard approached her. "Report to the main desk.
You'll pick up his personal effects and sign a release
form. Then he's free to go."

Wardy opened his mouth to say something, but, slowly standing up, his mother spoke first. "We'll talk in the car. *Not now.*" Her voice was like ice.

"How'd you find me?" he asked, breaking an uncomfortable silence as they drove home. Even to himself, his voice sounded dead. All he wanted to do was lie back and sleep. Block it all out.

"Mrs. O'Brien. Barry's mother. She called me, so I called the police." His mother was quiet. At least she didn't seem to want to chew him out. Surprising—his mother at a loss for words. "What else could I do? You were gone and I was afraid—afraid for your life. Can you understand that?" She paused again. "No, I guess you can't. There's no way you could feel the panic of a woman alone—alone and responsible for a runaway child. Wardy, this is…you've made everything—the separation, your coming home from military school—so much more difficult."

Wardy cleared his throat. He hadn't considered his mother's feelings when he'd hitched out of town— hadn't thought about anything except getting away. Even though he knew he should show some remorse, he had to ask an all-important question. "So, where am I going? Home with you—or to Dad's?" His heart thudded dully as he waited for her answer.

"Your father can't be bothered with you," she said tiredly. "It would interfere with all his plans to be a swinging single again. He doesn't want you now. You're coming home—with me."

****

"Tell me everything. Right from the beginning." Grandma Lou settled her pleasant, plump form back against the cushions of the studio couch. She took a long drink from her V-8 juice, then set the glass on the table, folded her arms, and turned expectantly to her grandson. "I'm truly sorry I wasn't here when you needed me most, but I'm here now, ready to make amends." Brushing back a lock of silvery hair, she tilted her head and leaned forward slightly. It was her way of saying, "Okay, now you have my undivided attention. I'm ready to listen; I'm going to understand."

Wardy loved these sessions with Grandma Lou. Ever since he could remember, they'd been having long talks on the beach house porch, all snug and glassed in, with plushy pillows and couches covered in dark blue denim, and a soft rag rug on the wood floor. Right now he could gaze out the large-paned windows and watch the gray, early winter sea, flat as sheet metal on the horizon. Now and then a fine spray of ocean shot straight up from the bleak shore, brushing the slate sky like an artist's delicate stroke.

Drawing up his knees and resting his chin on them, Wardy searched for a good starting place. "I guess it began the first day of the fall term at Martin-Barrett. They assigned me a room with the CC—the corridor chief, Kevin Kiser—and he was on my case from the start." Wardy swallowed hard, then went on. "Then there was the head meeting…" On and on he talked—about his dismissal from military school, about the bullies, his classes at Evanstown High and his experience with Mr. Guterman. Other than a sympathetic nod or two, there was no response from his grandmother, but she was taking it all in. Wardy knew that from past experience. She'd remember every word, every nuance, and when he was done, she'd help him sort out his feelings. She was the only one who'd ever been able—or willing—to do that.

They sat in companionable silence for a while. Then Grandma Lou reached for her glass again, and Wardy knew she was ready to talk. "That's quite a story, Wardy. A fairly direct descent since we talked last, huh? I think my art exhibition took me too far away—for too long."

Wardy nodded. He leaned back against the cushions, watching twilight glow on the sea. A gray-and-white gull, still as a statue, perched on an aged piling.

"You may be surprised at what I'm going to tell you," Grandma Lou continued, "but I think it's time you knew something about your old grandma here. It could help illuminate your present predicament—give us both a little insight." She brushed back her hair again. "When I was about your age, just going into high school, everybody insisted I was bright and gifted and capable of doing anything I wanted to. That's what they *said*. But when it came time for Lou to express some ideas and preferences, the People in Power insisted a mere slip of a girl like me was incapable of deciding her own destiny."

Intently, Wardy watched his grandmother's face. She had never told him much about her youth before, and he tried to picture her at his age.

"I'd always been artistic; however, I wanted to pursue a science career, be a paleontologist and work in an important museum—or be an archeologist in remote Africa. I would need a PhD degree, a small consideration to my mind. I knew what I wanted for my future. But the People in Power wouldn't hear of it. With my gift for art, they felt I should go to art school and get my fine arts degree. What I wanted was of no consequence, apparently. So, unconvinced and reluctant, I did what my parents and teachers expected. Even though I'd taken all the science courses in high school and excelled in them. I went to art school instead of Polytech, where I really longed to go. I got my degree in art."

She paused to take a breath. Wardy had never dreamed there'd been a rebellious side to Grandma Lou. To him, she had always seemed perfectly attuned to life—happy and satisfied. "Then what?" he asked.

"Then a funny thing happened." She laughed shortly. "I discovered I loved my art major. I'd determined that I wanted to paint for a living. I would create beauty, and my work would give pleasure wherever I went."

"So that's what you did, right? It all worked out, after all, didn't it?"

"No actually, Wardy, it was the same old story. Chapter Two. Once again, I allowed the Pretenders in my life to take over and make all the important decisions for me."

"Pretenders?"

"Yes. Pretenders. Those who pretended to know more about what was right and good for me than I knew myself. My father, for example, and my faculty advisor at art school. Even the dean of students, whom I have never forgiven to this day. They all insisted that my goals and ideals were unreachable for a woman—even a bright and talented one like me. They wanted me to *teach* art instead of creating art. They said teaching was a career compatible with marriage and motherhood—which they assumed I and all the women of my generation held uppermost in life." She grimaced. "I think, too, they questioned my determination, my tolerance for failure, my willingness to fight for success. An artist's life is not an easy one."

"So you did what they wanted. You became an art teacher. But you were good at it. You liked teaching, didn't you?"

"I hated it. It took me ten long years, but I knew I would never overcome the feeling I was wasting my God-given talent—missing out on what I really wanted from life. I quit teaching then, despite dire warnings from everyone, and took off on my own—rented a loft and began painting landscapes."

"And you were successful. You were happy then."

His grandmother smiled. "Oh, it was a hard life. There were times I wanted to give up—to return to the security of a regular paycheck. But I never considered going back after that—not really. I guess you'd say my life was one long war, skirmish after skirmish, until I had the guts to do what I finally knew was right for me."

"Well, you sure fooled everybody."

"No, I didn't fool *everybody*. Ask my first husband. Or my second one." She chuckled. "You might also talk to the people at Alcoholics Anonymous. They could tell you how many people I fooled in my life."

"You mean you were . . .you were an alcoholic?" Wardy couldn't believe it. He had never seen his grandmother drink anything stronger than grape juice.

"Not *was*. *Am*. I am what is called a recovering alcoholic, meaning I'm cured of alcoholism as long as I never take another drink." She pointed to the V-8 juice. "But let's draw parallels, now. I can see a pattern already evolving in your life. The struggle between you and the Pretenders in your world."

"I'm only a kid. Nobody will listen to my side. They've all got their own ideas about how I'm going to act and what I have to do. Just like when you were a kid, huh?"

"Sometimes you *have* to act the way they want you to. There's no sense causing friction over social conventions or society's interpretation of polite behavior. It's too inconsequential to get hung up on, and the easiest part of all is to behave yourself, be polite. Remember, bullies like Jimmo Rogers choose to pounce on kids who stand out because they're different. If you act out—react to their taunts—you exaggerate the difference they already sense in you. But that's not all I'm talking about. What I mean is, you can't let the Pretenders make the decisions that might ruin your chances for happiness, as I did. You know what you love to do and what you want to do. So *do* it. *Be* it. Don't let anyone stop you. Listen to Shakespeare: 'To thine own self be true.' "

For a moment Wardy didn't say anything. At last he ventured, "I think I know what you're saying, what you feel I should do. I'll try. But it's not going to be easy. At school, everybody seems to have me pigeonholed already."

"Just remember me. I spent years battling with myself and others to find out what was really right for me. But when I knew—when I knew who I was and what I wanted—I went for it, against all the odds. I've been a happy woman ever since. Don't make the same mistakes I did." She hugged him fiercely. "And if you want to be a lab assistant, go for it. Get another interview with that German fellow, what was his name? Guterman. Don't let anything stop you."

They both stood up. "Wardy, one more thing before you go. Don't believe everything your mother tells you about your dad. Ward really tried to bring you up right. All those teams he kept putting you on—he wanted you to know how to handle yourself with your peers. It might have worked, too, but your mother—my daughter—always wanted the upper hand with you. She invented excuse after excuse for you: allergies, asthma, your size. You name it. I think she was secretly afraid your father would succeed with you—make you not need her anymore—and take you away from her, from her control. I've no doubt the pulling and pushing your parents put you through in your early years contributed to some of your problems now. Psychologists call it 'mixed signals.' Anyway, it's bound to confuse a youngster. You're old enough to know that, I think." She reached for her empty glass. "Now. I'd better get out to the kitchen, or there'll be no Thanksgiving turkey for tomorrow."

Wardy watched her leave. Without thinking, he let himself out the back door and strolled down the rickety wooden walkway to the beach. Though the sea air was damp, cold, there was a cleanness, a naturalness to it. When he breathed, his lungs grew stronger and larger, renewed. Walking along the shore, he scuffed sand with the toes of his running shoes and mulled over Grandma Lou's advice.

She's right. I'm letting everybody make decisions about the important things because I'm so hung up on the unimportant ones. The way I let the kids at school get to me. Mom and Dad. Leslie. Well, no more. I'm going to pass biology so I can take chemistry. Physics. I'll go back and talk to Mr. Guterman again. Build my laser. Be a real scientist. Ward M. Spinks, Jr., nuclear physicist. Me. The real me.

A twinge of guilt hovered over the edge of his thoughts. Grandma Lou had shared details about her difficult past, told him her innermost feelings, but he hadn't leveled with her completely. He hadn't told her about the letterhead stationery from Quick-Print—how he wanted to write, acting as a science professor to get expert advice on his laser. First, he wanted to try sending some letters to see what would happen, see if anybody would respond to his queries. His grandmother would never approve of such dishonesty, but he had to try. It was so important—even more important now that he'd hit on a workable fuel for his laser. Hexafluoride. That's what he was going to use. Hexafluoride.

Chapter Seven

He'd made up his mind to see Mr. Guterman today about the job of lab assistant. Grandma Lou's talk had sunk in, made him realize what he really wanted. That was why he rode his bike instead of the school bus—so he could stay after school and go to Mr. Guterman's office. As of last week the sign was still in place on the bulletin board, and, meticulous as Mr. Guterman must be, Wardy was sure it meant the job was still open. Maybe everybody else was as afraid of the teacher as he was. As he locked his bike into the rack, his attention was drawn to a knot of students gathered around the wooden picnic tables in the quad. They wielded their phones, laughing, stroking and tapping their screens, eagerly showing them to each other. You weren't allowed to activate your cell phone inside the school building; everybody shut them down with the opening bell each morning, so it wasn't unusual to see a lot of phone use here outside school. But you didn't often see kids sharing in such numbers. Solitude was the nature of today's electronic communications. Just me and my phone. In the gathering crowd, he recognized Jocko and Jimmo of the Marx Brothers. He sensed whatever electronic messaging was going on, it involved him.

Slowly, he made his way around the side of the school, hoping to avoid recognition. He kept close to the wall and inched along near the shrubbery. Mr. Harris, the assistant principal, would be on the scene shortly, Wardy knew. He had a knack for breaking up mob scenes. In the meantime, the laughing, jostling crowd was growing. Slinking around the side of the building so he could slip in the back door, Wardy found himself face-to-face with Jocko Osbourne.

"Ea-gle-bait, Ea-gle-bait, Ea-gle-bait," Jocko chanted, holding up a smartphone so that Wardy could view a Facebook page there. *Eaglebait Fan Page* it read. Wardy could see all kinds of posts: "Dweeb!" said one. "Go back to military school," another. "Short, fat geek." He'd seen enough. Wardy whipped around him, moving quickly on, but Jocko did not follow. *Probably figures he'll have more fun out there watching the crowd reaction.* Wardy paused inside the door. He didn't subscribe to Facebook himself, but he knew lots of kids did. Social networking, they called it. Ganging up on losers was more like it. Instant bullying. Slumping, scuffing his feet, with lowered head, he proceeded to his locker.

I'm off to a great start. Take charge of my life. Ignore the creeps. Ha. They network me as Eaglebait, the enemy, and the whole school gets a good laugh. How do I ignore that? Why can't they just let me alone?

Jamming his coat and lunch into his locker, he headed for his first class. As he wound through the maze of students in the hallways, he could hear buzzing laughter. They were talking about him hanging out there in cyberspace, he knew that. He wanted to scream out, tell them all to leave him alone—but he didn't.

Ignore them. Ignore them. I'm going to run my own life. Forget the unimportant things. Sticks and stones.

It was the slowest morning of his life. In every class

people sneaked peeks at him, pointing him out, whispering to each other, "There's the fella on Facebook. What a loser." He ate his solitary lunch in the restroom. Nobody would be in there for at least fifteen minutes when the lunch lines closed, except for the smokers, and they would only be interested in a quick puff. He'd be safe for a little while, at least. Once sounds of students in the halls began, Wardy slipped out the door and took the long way around to Latin class. Sneaking around was becoming second nature. He didn't want to risk running into any of his antagonists.

Quietly, he entered the Latin room. Mrs. Burnett wrote on the board, her back to him, too absorbed, and, possibly, too deaf, to hear him enter. Wardy's heart leapt when he realized the only other student in the room was Meg Reilly, his biology lab partner. Of all people. He wanted to slide under the desk and crawl out of the room. But, too late. She had seen him and was watching him from her desk across the room. Shyly, tentatively, she smiled, giving a tiny wave of her hand. Was it a genuine smile? Or the snickering, jeering smile he'd been getting all day? It seemed sweet enough, but why? Why would a beautiful girl like Meg Reilly be smiling at the joke of the school? Mrs. Burnett scratched away busily at the board, oblivious to them both.

Again, Wardy felt an urge to flee. He had longed to talk to Meg—worshiped her for weeks—but why on this day of ridiculous humiliation, why did she have to be alone in the classroom with him? He could feel his cheeks burn with shame.

Meg caught his eye. She placed a finger to her lips, signaling silence. Then she slid an amused glance at the teacher's back. Wardy nodded dumbly, his agitation increasing. She was so pretty. Her soft brown hair curled around her narrow cheeks, and when she smiled, her warm brown eyes glowed beneath perfectly arched brows.

With the ringing of the bell, students began to push through the door. Mrs. Burnett turned around with a vague jolt of surprise. "Oh. Time for class, I see." Meg winked and smiled again.

Wardy tried to concentrate on the derivatives Mrs. Burnett harped on, but Meg's sweet attention had destroyed his mental discipline. His thoughts drifted until, almost without realizing it, he found himself scratching laser fuel formulas on the side of his Latin worksheet. He'd cross one out and begin anew. Before he knew it, he was completely immersed in equations.

"Mr. Spinks? Could we have your attention back here on earth?" The Latin teacher could be acerbic at times. The class tittered. Wardy grimaced. He hadn't the slightest idea what question Mrs. Burnett had asked him.

"Sorry," he muttered. "I wasn't listening." Again the class rippled. *Why? Why does Meg have to be in here to hear this? She must think I'm a complete buffoon.* At last the bell rang to end class. Wardy held back so he would be the last to leave; he'd discovered it was safer that way. But he wondered about Meg Reilly. *She's so soft. And beautiful. And nice. I think I'm in love.*

His thoughts carried him all the way through biology class as he sat beside Meg at the lab table. He had never had the nerve to speak with her about anything except lab work; it was all business, no small talk. It seemed odd to Wardy that Meg never ventured to change their formal kind of relationship. The final bell of the day brought him back to reality with a feeling of panic. Mr.

Guterman. He meant to apply for the lab assistant position again. Walking down the hall, he rehearsed over and over what he would say, how he would say it. *I can do it, Mr. G. I know I can. I've had the experience.* Halting in front of the closed office door, from within, he could hear the low murmur of voices. Guterman! Was he interviewing someone else? Wardy raised his hand to knock. His heart pounded through his rib cage. Swallowing his courage, he turned and headed in the opposite direction. It had been too exhausting a day already. He couldn't face any more humiliation, rejection. He'd try again. Tomorrow. When things were calmer.

****

Wardy's mother had a late appointment, and Leslie was sleeping over at a friend's house. "I won't be home until after ten," his mother told him on the phone.

It was the opportunity he'd been hoping for. He glanced at his watch. There would be four uninterrupted hours to complete his experiment, an experiment for which he needed the microwave oven. Taking a deep breath, he set to work. He brought all his needed materials and equipment up from the lab and laid them out on the kitchen table. *Good old Junior Wizard Chemistry Set.* he opened the hinged doors to the kit. *If you only knew what's in store for you tonight.* Reaching into a paper bag, he drew out the green plastic squeeze bottle of Florahex, a common antiseptic he'd bought at the drugstore. Working carefully, he distilled and concentrated the hexafluoride from the antiseptic. Then he cautiously opened a vial of nitric acid and mixed it with the hexafluoride in a glass container. Everything was proceeding on schedule. Sealing the glass container, he crossed to the microwave on the kitchen counter. *Ha! I'll bet they don't have a recipe for this in Mom's microwave cookbook.* He closed the door and set the dial for thirty minutes.

"I'll set it for another thirty minutes after I've checked the solution," he said aloud. "While that's cooking, I think I'll write down the formula." He went to work with pencil and paper at the kitchen table, so absorbed that the ding of the timer startled him, *Now. Thirty more minutes and the chef will emerge with the winning entrée,* he congratulated himself.

The time had come. With shaking hands, he opened the door to the oven and observed the glass container. *Better let it cool. Now all I have to do is set this compound inside the laser tube and energize it.* The molecules in the compound had become metastable—a population inversion. Like pumping air into a balloon. The more you squeezed in, the louder the pop when it blew.

Carefully carrying the glass container to his basement lab, Wardy reviewed the process he would have to carry out for a successful experiment. Once he got the substance inside the laser tube, he planned to use a strobe light to activate it. *Lucky for me Dad left his timing light when he split. The strobe in that tool should work perfectly on my laser.*

All was ready. *Well, here goes.* Picking up the timing light, he aimed the muzzle into the laser tube. Then, taking a deep breath, he pulled the trigger, and jumped back. Instantly there was a long flash—a pure, bright, intense violet flash that glowed as it moved at the speed of light, back and forth, back and forth, inside the glass casing until it shot out both ends of the tube in a powerful beam. Amazed, awed, Wardy watched as two big holes, one in each wall of the lab, appeared as if blasted by magic.

"It works!" he screamed in delight. "My laser works! What power! Two holes in the walls!" One at a time he examined them. Then he appraised his laser—or the remains of it. *Well, I knew it would be a one-shot laser. Destroys itself. Have to start all over again. But I have it down on paper. I know how to do it.* Tingling with elation, he estimated the level of destruction to the lab walls. Tomorrow he'd get out the spackle compound and repair them. It was a good thing Dad was giving him a hefty allowance now. He toted up the expenses of the night's experiment. Then he remembered to check his watch.

"Holy cow! Got to get the kitchen cleaned up before Mom comes home," he reminded himself. Wardy dashed up the stairs two at a time, went to the kitchen table, and scooped up his materials and equipment, placing everything in a big box. Then he wiped the table and counters clean. At the last minute, he thought to give the microwave a swipe with the sponge, too. If Mom knew he was cooking hexafluoride and nitric acid in her oven, she'd be furious. Finally, he was satisfied the kitchen appeared neat as always. He'd deal with the lab tomorrow. Turning off the kitchen light, he headed for his room.

Locking the door, Wardy moved to his desk. Pulling out the bottom drawer, he reached under the false bottom he'd built some years ago for secret documents. He drew out a list he'd made after an Internet search—a list of research scientists and university professors specializing in laser technology. From the same secret spot came a sheet of Quick-Print letterhead paper.

WARD M. SPINKS, JR., PhD

Professor of

Nuclear Physics

Wardy began his first letter. He had completely forgotten about the Facebook "fan" page.

Chapter Eight

Whitcomb cleared his throat, standing before the students as they waited for him to speak. "Well, class, since school is about to wind up before the winter holiday, I've saved my news for this opportune moment."

It was like Whitcomb to throw in a few big words for the GT class. *What a pompous pigeon.*

"After-much soul-searching and all due consideration, I have come to a decision."

He's so smug. Why doesn't he get on with it? Wardy was bored with the whole business. Just like any other day in old Whitcomb's bio class. Boring. He stopped listening.

"...for the remainder of the school term I will be taking a position in England—as an exchange teacher. The principal and I have worked out what we think is an equitable solution to the problem of a substitute for me."

A substitute? Wardy pricked up his ears. *No more Whitcomb? Hallelujah!*

". . and it's been decided that Mr. Heinrich Guterman, who's on loan to us from Germany this year, will take over my classes. Mr. Guterman's current schedule is being shifted around to accommodate this plan. That's pronounced *Goo-ter-man*, for the uninformed."

Whitcomb paused, waiting for feedback from the

students. Wardy would give him feedback. He'd be the first to wish Whitcomb bon voyage. The rest of the class buzzed. Mr. Guterman had already acquired quite a reputation at Evanstown High. Wardy was well aware of that. Hadn't he tried twice more to apply for the lab assistant's position, only to get cold feet and back out right before the teacher's office door? Everybody said Guterman was brilliant, but impossible—a great teacher, but a perfectionist. A stern taskmaster.

The bell rang. Wardy stacked and restacked his books. Guterman taking over Whitcomb's classes. What would it mean for him? Would it be a chance to get into some advanced material—a resource for his own projects? The laser?

He realized that all the other students had departed, all, that is, except for Meg Reilly, who stood beside him at the lab table. They were alone in the room. Panic grabbed him. She was so quiet; he hadn't realized she was still there. He ought to say something to her. After all, she had kind of opened the communication lines in Latin class. But that had been a while back, and she was so reserved it was hard to read her. Something of a loner, too. She never rushed out the door at the end of the day to gather with the sheep like the other brainless kids in his class. He swallowed the lump in his throat.

"Wow. That was some announcement, huh?" He almost jumped at the sound of his own voice, surprised at his nerve. He was actually talking to Meg about something other than biology.

"What?" Her voice was whisper-soft, mildly surprised—as if she had not expected Wardy to talk to her. "Oh, Yes. I wonder what he'll be like, Mr. Goo-ter-man." She put just enough emphasis on Whitcomb's pronunciation to make it comical.

Wardy laughed. Relief spread across him in a calming wave, replacing his nervousness. All of a sudden he wanted to talk to this beautiful lab partner of his, really connect with her. It was as though a door of silence had been unlocked with a secret key, not at all like working on labs together. Did Meg feel it, too? "Some of those German scientists are really brilliant. Their technology's right up with ours—maybe even more advanced," he said.

"So I've read." Her voice was still hushed and whispery.

"Maybe he'll be a fantastic teacher—somebody who'll understand what we want to learn about . . ." Wardy trailed off.

"Let's face it, anybody would be better than Mr. Whitcomb."

Wardy regarded her with amazement. "You mean you don't like him either? I figured I was the only one."

Meg laughed—a silvery bell tinkling. "He's such an elitist. Would he ever let a day go by without reminding us how privileged we are to be 'gifted and talented'? Some of us are tired of being singled out, for being labeled. We don't need daily reminders."

Wardy wondered if she knew what a sensitive chord she had struck. Was it possible that this beautiful, self-possessed girl felt as isolated, as different, as he did? No. It couldn't be true.

For a moment, Meg was silent, as if deciding whether to continue the conversation or not. Then she began again in her whispery voice. "Have you ever been in one of the SL centers?"

"SL? What's that?"

"SL stands for *superior learner*. That's the tippy-top of the gifted strata. They take the SLs out of the regular school GT programs and bus them off to centers where everything is very high-level and academic. And competitive. So competitive that nobody ever has a chance to make any real friends. You never know when you're going to be pitted against someone else for a summer scholarship or a travel grant or the Governor's School for the Gifted. It's like one big all-year-long College Bowl quiz game to see who can rack up the most points and win the prize. Some of the kids eat it up, but not me."

Meg went silent as they exited the room. Wardy heard the last bus bell and knew he'd have to walk home. But he didn't care. He'd have been willing to walk ten miles for an opportunity to talk with Meg Reilly. He wanted desperately to keep her talking.

"I take it you were in an SL center," he said as they walked down the hall.

Meg sighed, started to speak, then signed again. "For three years. Three miserable years, until my parents saw how unhappy I was. That was last year—they took me out, suggested I come to Evanstown—thought it might help . . .my problems."

"You must have very understanding parents. Most of them would probably kill to have their children in an SL center."

"They could see I was so unhappy it was making me ill, physically ill, I mean. I stopped eating and cried all the time." Appearing embarrassed, she became silent.

Wardy longed to return to the happier shared moments at the start of their conversation, but he didn't know how to steer things back. Perhaps, sensing his feelings, she shrugged her shoulders as if ridding herself of unpleasant memories. She smiled a little thinly.

"Anyway, this is my first year back in a neighborhood school. I still don't know many people. Sometimes I feel they figure me for an egghead—a brain or something." With another wan smile, she continued. "I'm so much happier here than I was with the constant pressure of the center, I don't care. Every day is a pleasure."

They had reached the end of the hall outside the biology room. The corridors were deserted and quiet. "Well, guess I'd better get going," Meg said. "My mother's picking me up today. We're going Christmas shopping right after school." She started to go, then turned and said, "Bye, Wardy."

It was the first time she'd said his name, and it sent shivers up his spine. The red turtleneck sweater turned up under her chin made her cheeks glow and served as a contrast to the fine brown hair feathering down onto her shoulders. She was the picture of beauty—a goddess—and she was smiling at him, Wardy Spinks. Was it possible, or was it a dream?

For some reason, he became tongue-tied. "B-Bye, Meg," he stammered. "See y' around." He waved, but she had already turned her back, walking away. *I love you. You're beautiful and I love you.*

****

There were two letters for him in the mail. One, he figured, was from Barry. It came in a green envelope like a Christmas card. But the other? Could it be? Was it an answer to one of his letterhead letters? He bolted up the stairs to his room, locked the door, and, with shaking fingers, tore open the long, cream-colored business envelope. *Robert M. Lowry, PhD*, the letterhead read. He scanned the letter with mounting excitement.

Dear Dr. Spinks:

Re: your letter of November 21, I am intrigued by several aspects of your laser experimentation. Laser design is an area with which my laboratory has been concerned recently. We have experimented with several mirror shapes and arrangements that I am happy to share with a colleague in exchange for further information. Enclosed are several designs I think you will find usable. I might further suggest cooling the mirrors with a pure, high-quality oil. This will make them last longer and help them retain their shape.

I am most interested in the following aspects of your experiments: First, how did you derive the compound medium for your laser? Would you be willing to share your formulas? Also, what wattage did your laser beam produce?

I extend, of course, all professional courtesy regarding your research. You will be given credit for any data used by our laboratory in successful experiments. I trust our designs will be helpful in your work and hope to hear from you again.

Sincerely,

Robert M. Lowry, Ph.D.

Wardy read the letter again and again. Dr. Lowry's lab was connected with a university and research facility in California. It had been the very first name on the list he'd compiled off the Internet. What luck! And the professor had provided an e-mail address. Wardy couldn't wait to try out the mirror designs. Linseed oil. That's what he'd use to coat the mirrors. He already had a bottle on hand in the lab. Of course, he'd send Dr.

Lowry the formulas and wattage. What better way to keep the correspondence going? Only, he didn't know what the wattage on his laser was. He had no idea. Strong enough to blow big holes in the walls was all he knew for sure. How could he measure laser wattage? That problem would take some work.

Sitting down at his desk, he booted up his computer to email Dr. Lowry. He bent to his task.

A sharp knock sounded on the door, sending him straight out of his chair. He went to the door and opened it a crack. It was his mother. "What?" he asked in an annoyed voice.

"Beg your pardon," his mother said with an edge of sarcasm to her voice. "Could you open the door a trifle more?"

With a nervous glance at the letter on his desk, Wardy complied hesitantly.

His mother took in the cluttered room. "When are you going to clean up this pigsty?"

"Is that why you knocked?"

"No. Actually, I wanted to tell you that Grandma Lou is coming for the holidays. On the other hand, if you expect to entertain her in this room, you'd *better* consider cleaning it up."

It was on the tip of his tongue: Grandma Lou never judged him by the condition of his surroundings. But there was no sense in generating another fight with his mother. "Social convention," Grandma Lou called it, he remembered. "Okay, I'll clean it up. Tomorrow. When does she get in?"

"Tomorrow night. She has an exhibit in the city she wants to check out, and she'll come over here right after. She'll be staying a week." His mother's eyes swept the room again, and, with a final sigh of resignation, she went out the door.

Grandma Lou. Great. Should he show her the letter from Dr. Lowry? How would she react? Would she be outraged at his duplicity or delighted with his ingenuity? He couldn't decide. Still mulling over thoughts of Dr. Lowry and Grandma Lou, he picked up the green envelope and opened it. It was from Barry, as he'd suspected. Underneath his signature on the Santa Claus card he'd scrawled a message. *"Sorry about the police in Raleigh. My mom caught Rob and me going out to the car, and she got the story out of us. She called your mom. I heard about the cops later. Maybe I'll be seeing you soon anyway."* What did he mean by that?

****

Grandma Lou came bustling in the next night, rosy-cheeked, bright-eyed, and laden with colorfully wrapped packages. "It's a very good show," she enthused. "I'm one of six artists displaying paintings. There've been good crowds—lots of interest, according to my agent. What a thrilling experience for an old horse like me—to see my work on display!" As she talked, she unloaded package after package onto the table. "Do we have to wait 'til Christmas to open the gifts?" She directed the question to her daughter, but she sounded more like the child than the mother—or the grandmother. Excitement sparkled in her eyes. Ever since Wardy could remember, every Christmas she'd asked the same question: "Do we have to wait?"

Gwen laughed. "Can't you at least take your coat off, Mom?"

"Oh, goody! I just want to see if you like what I've brought." Grandma Lou clapped her hands together in glee, ripped her coat and gloves off, and started handing out packages.

Every year she managed to come up with the right gifts. They weren't always terribly expensive, but they were perfect. Wardy opened his first package; a thick, dark green beach towel embossed with a ferocious orange tiger decorating the middle. It was the coolest beach towel he'd ever seen. He thought he might hang it on the wall of his room. And then a battery-operated device that looked like a watch. It measured steps and miles walked, heart rate, and all kinds of other things. Best of all was the last gift. When he removed the paper wrapping, he saw that the box was from Radio Depot, but he knew it wasn't a radio. "Photocell" was written on the box. Ripping open the end of the box, he discovered a black, rectangular object that resembled a movie camera.

"What's a photocell?"

"I figure a scientist like you could find all kinds of uses for a photocell."

"Photocell—you mean an electric eye?"

"Yes. Like a burglar alarm. It measures the brightness of light," Grandma Lou said, and Wardy remembered his grandmother had been a whiz at science herself.

His mind was working. It measures the brightness of light. The brightness of light...the laser! He could use the photocell to determine the watt power generated by his laser. He knew he could!

"Grandma Lou," he told her, releasing her from a bear hug, "you've done it again!" He dashed for the basement stairs with the photocell under his arm, leaving his grandmother and mother to stare, wordless, after him.

"Now what do you suppose he meant by that?" Grandma Lou asked her daughter as Wardy disappeared from view.

"Who knows?" Gwen shrugged. "Who knows what he does in that room in the basement?"

Chapter Nine

A muted buzz hovered over the biology room. *Something's up. Something more than the arrival of Heinrich Guterman, the new teacher. I hope the class clowns don't ruin it for the guy before he has a chance.*

The door opened. The buzzing stopped, replaced by a gasp. Many of the students had not realized how strikingly handsome the teacher was. Framed in the doorway with the light behind his blonde head, he seemed to glow with a godlike presence. *"Guten Tag,"* he said in his clear, modulated voice.

Mr. Guterman strode to the head of the class and placed his briefcase on the desk. He carried a tan-colored trench coat folded over his arm. Spying a cupboard in a corner, he pulled open the left-hand door, then drew back, startled. The class was dead silent. Suspended from the horizontal pole across the top of the closet was a full human skeleton from the physiology lab next door. Pinned to its chest bones was a sign: This Is What Happens to Eaglebait. Wardy felt his chest heat up. He lowered his gaze to the table, afraid to catch Meg's eye. *It's the Marx Brothers again. Or one of their beefy friends in here. Jocko and Jimmo—always ready with a joke.*

The class sat tensely, waiting for Mr. Guterman's reaction. Without missing a beat, just loud enough to be heard by everyone, he said, "I see. One of Mr.

Whitcomb's old students. He failed the course, no doubt." Hanging his coat beside the skeleton, he shut the door.

The class roared with laughter. Mr. Guterman had passed the test. *And they put another one over on me.* Wardy thought ruefully. Every eye was on the new teacher now. He'd gotten their attention, all right.

"I understand that this is an accelerated class." It was more of a statement than a question. Wardy and Meg's eyes met briefly. Was this to be a repeat of Whitcomb's ideas on how to teach the gifted? But Mr. Guterman spoke again in that cultivated tone with the slight trace of a German accent. "I am of the opinion that accelerated classes, like all others, must first master the basics. However, once accomplished, we can proceed at the fastest pace possible. There are no limits to learning when it comes to science." Mr. Guterman stressed the sibilant sounds in his words.

Wardy inhaled with excitement. Maybe the teacher wouldn't resent his desire for knowledge beyond the text, the way Whitcomb seemed to. Maybe he would even help Wardy carry out some of his experiments. No. Better not think too far ahead. That could lead to bitter disappointment.

Mr. Guterman continued, "I would like to find out what you know about biology—about science. This is a diagnostic tool. Use the rest of the class period to answer these questions as completely and accurately as you can." He began passing out papers to the rows of students.

Wardy concentrated on the first page. It was unlike any diagnostic he had ever taken. There were all sorts of questions—some factual, some opinion, some problem-solving. All thought-provoking, Wardy realized. It was hard to grasp just what Guterman was after, so vaguely worded were some of the questions. For the first time that year, Wardy threw all his energy into an assignment. He wasn't sure why he was so enthusiastic about the task, but it had something to do with Mr. Guterman—his aura, his commanding presence. Wardy wanted to impress the man—to succeed. When the bell rang, he was still writing. The room had emptied out by the time Wardy approached Mr. Guterman's desk to hand him the papers. The teacher smiled, revealing very straight, white teeth. Once again Wardy realized the man was quite handsome. The girls were in ecstasy, no doubt.

"Hmm." Mr. Guterman pointed to Wardy's name on the paper. "Wardy Spinks. I believe you interviewed for the position of lab assistant some time ago." His eyes locked into Wardy's again. "Though the interview was short, I thought you had possibilities. I was surprised when you did not return to discuss those possibilities. Very surprised."

Wardy found himself speechless. He had considered the entire interview a failure. Why was Guterman surprised he hadn't pursued it further? What was it about this man that intrigued him so, yet intimidated him at the same time?

The teacher continued to talk in a conversational tone. "Would this be in reference to you?" Mr. Guterman showed Wardy the flip side of the Eaglebait sign hung around the skeleton's neck. *Warty Spinks Is Eaglebait*, it read. "Warty Spinks. Wardy. You?"

Wardy ducked his head. "They don't like me much, I guess," he mumbled.

"Why not, Wardy Spinks?"

Wardy shrugged. "Because I'm ugly and fat and not athletic."

"And you always rise to the bait," Mr. Guterman said evenly. "Pun, would you say?"

Again, Wardy shrugged. "Usually, I guess. It's hard to ignore them all the time."

Very slowly Mr. Guterman nodded, his eyes riveted on Wardy. "Perhaps we can do something to counteract that, Wardy Spinks. Would you like that?"

Stunned by the turn of the conversation, Wardy nodded mutely, then turned back to gather up his books.

Numbly, he made his way out the door into the hall where Meg waited for him. Sometimes, after biology, the last class of the day, they would stroll down the hall and talk. Whatever had broken the communication dam between them, Wardy was grateful for the closeness their new relationship afforded. But today he wasn't sure he wanted to face her with the heat of his humiliation still smoldering deep inside. Everybody in class knew that skeleton was another joke on him.

"Hi, Meg," he said weakly.

"I just wanted you to know that not everybody goes along with that Eaglebait stuff. It's a cruel joke. Some people don't approve of cruelty. And the Facebook Eaglebait page…it's disgusting." She gazed at him with her big eyes. Honesty was all he saw—no pity.

Wardy felt himself melting under her spell. "Thanks. It's okay. I'm trying to learn not to rise to the bait. Pun intended."

They walked off down the hall together.

****

Wardy finally had the house to himself again. He'd been itching to try the photocell on his newest laser, but he hadn't forgotten the holes in the wall from the last go-round. Ready with a fresh batch of hexafluoride, Wardy made a critical evaluation of the reconstructed laser, appraising the long glass tube with mirrors at both ends. He'd followed Dr. Lowry's suggestions for this latest set of mirrors—placed them so that they were parallel, one partially transparent and one fully reflective. He'd coated them with linseed oil to help cool them, and arranged them as nearly like Dr. Lowry's diagrams as possible. His mouth went dry with nervousness. Now he knew how athletes on the starting blocks at the Olympics must feel—rapid pulse, shallow breathing, and parched mouth.

Dr. Lowry had responded to Wardy's e-mail, repeating his request for the watt power of the laser. So, this was the test, the all-important test. Picking up the photocell, Wardy gave it a loving pat. "Can't place you directly in the path of the beam, fella," he said to the photocell, "or you'd be blasted into a million pieces." He picked up a piece of glass and positioned it. "Got to use this glass at an angle to index the refraction of light—check out the amount of light that goes through and the amount refracted. Then I can estimate the watt power. I hope." He talked out loud to himself, internalizing Dr. Lowry's instructions.

He checked and rechecked. It was as ready as it would ever be. Still nervous, Wardy lifted the timing light. "Here goes." After checking the position of the glass and the photocell one last time, he aimed the strobe, fighting an urge to squeeze his eyes shut. Purple light flared inside the tube, then shot out. BOOM! This time the corrected mirrors had trapped the laser into one-way direction. Now there was a hole in only one wall—but it was twice as big! And the photocell, as well as the glass tube, had remained intact. He made some quick calculations. NO—that couldn't be right. He forced himself to slow down, recalculated, then whistled. "Holy cow! Dr. Lowry will never believe it. I've constructed a laser with 500 watts of power. Over 250,000 times the power of the ShopRite scanner I started with!"

Gingerly, he fingered the huge hole in the lab wall. There was a little smoke from the crushed cinder block, but no burning smell, thank goodness. *Boy, this is going to be something to fix. Good thing I waited until everybody was gone. Wonder how much longer I can get away with these experiments before the whole foundation topples? How much noise does it make outside the lab? Maybe I should build some steel reinforcements for the wall before I try this again.* But his elation far overshadowed his worry. His laser—all that power. Who would've thought it would be so powerful? It was like a tornado or a hurricane. Something that started out mild and, before you knew it, turned into a destructive force. *I'll name my laser—just like they name hurricanes. Violet—for the violet light that flares inside. You're Big Vi now, my friend Big Vi— my powerful friend hidden in my basement lab.*

As he picked up the debris from the shattered wall, he mentally composed the e-mail he would write to Dr. Lowry. *Dear Dr. Lowry: My latest experiment has enabled me to estimate the wattage of my laser at around 500 watts. I have used a photocell and calculated the refraction of light. However, I would be interested in learning how your lab measures watt power produced by laser beams. Incidentally, the mirror designs you suggested worked very well...* He dictated to himself happily as he worked.

On the way upstairs to his room he fingered the phone in his pocket. Wouldn't he like to call Meg now and hear her whispery voice? Would she talk to him over the phone the way she did after bio class? He felt his mouth go dry again at the thought. Shoot. Calling a girl on the phone would take more nerve than blasting a hole in the wall with his laser. A sudden thought occurred to him: *Guterman. What would the teacher think about Big Vi?* Wardy shook his head. *No. Not yet. Maybe someday, though.* The possibility sent shivers down his spine.

Tossing and turning amid knotted, snarled sheets, Wardy felt the threads of the past week wind through his consciousness like the strands of a spider's web. What had Guterman meant when he'd asked him, "Would you like that?" Wardy could recall the teacher's exact words and tone. "Perhaps we can do something to counteract that, Wardy Spinks. Would you like that?" What had he meant by "something"? And counteract what? The practical jokers? The jokes themselves? Wardy's own basic unpopularity? In and out, up and down, back and forth his thoughts crossed and re-crossed. Guterman was only an exchange teacher. What made him think he could do anything for Wardy? He was impressive, no doubt about it. A week in the classroom was enough to tell Wardy the man knew his stuff. Not just biology, either. Chemistry, physics, biophysics, and a lot more. The class was stimulating, charged with energy. Thoughts and ideas ignited like sparks in Guterman's class. He had completely different theories about GT classes than Whitcomb, all right. Whitcomb thought the students were elite because they were smart. Guterman thought learning opened limitless boundaries because the students' intelligence blasted away all the usual barriers. Nobody was elite in Guterman's class. Everybody sweated the same.

Sliding off the bed, he worked to rearrange the hopelessly tangled linens. When he climbed back at last into the cocoon of covers, he tried to relax his overcharged imagination. *Don't think about the laser. Don't think about Guterman. You'll be awake all night. Think about something soothing. Soft. Pretty. Is there any hope for me, Meg?*

Chapter Ten

Meg waited outside the biology room at the end of the day. It was the second time this week. Last week was the same. Wardy began to live for the end of each day, just to see if she would be there.

"Hi. I wondered if you wanted to work on the biology assignment in the library after school today." The whisper of her voice was a gentle breeze in the air.

Wardy slung his books over his hip. "Okay. Report's due in a week, right?"

They walked toward the library at a leisurely pace. "Lab's sure a lot more exciting with Guterman than it was with Whitcomb." He gave a short laugh. "I never thought I'd enjoy exploring frog guts."

"Exciting? I wouldn't call it that. I mean, if you've seen one aorta, you've seen them all. But it's definitely more fun."

Wardy gave her a sideways glimpse. "Don't tell me you've fallen under the spell of the German's aura like all the other girls in the class."

She grinned. "I must admit, the man's a hunk. But, seriously, I think what makes Guterman such a good teacher is the way he makes us do research and then discuss what we've learned. It opens up the field, in a way."

"Opens up. Ha! I like that. Opens up the frog— opens up the field." They reached the double doors to the library; automatically Wardy lowered his voice.

"I see a clear table in the corner." He pointed. "Let's sit there." He noticed a bank of students working at the computers and thought briefly about the *Eaglebait* page on Facebook. Students were blocked from using Facebook at school, but that didn't stop them from posting from their phones or their own computers at home. He knew the *Eaglebait* page was still going strong. The sly stares and whispered slurs followed him around school like a bad virus. He'd considered joining Facebook but didn't know if he could resist checking out the *Eaglebait* page. Didn't know if he could hold up under the barrage of insults he'd find there.

"I'll check the online *Reader's Guide* for the magazine articles," Meg offered, once they'd put down their books.

"All right. I'll get the books from the reference room."

For a while, they sat engrossed, reading. Suddenly Wardy raised his head. "Hey, check out this diagram. Do you think you could draw it for our report? Blow it up, maybe?"

Meg scrutinized the diagram. "I can replicate it in India ink. Do you think Guterman would like it?"

"We'll get five extra credit points for this jewel. Good thing art's one of your talents. I haven't got a clue when it comes to graphics." He paused. "You know, I can't believe this."

"Believe what?"

"We're staying after school, going to the library, jazzed about a dumb biology report. And liking it."

"Mr. Guterman's got us all under some kind of spell, I think." Her eyes widened.

"I know. We're not the only ones. Take a peek around this library—there're kids all over the place from bio class. What's come over everyone?"

Tilting her head, Meg appeared to be choosing her words carefully. "It's hard to pin down. Whitcomb was satisfied if you just memorized everything. But Guterman? Guterman says facts are only the beginning."

Wardy put on a false accent. "Critical thinking. Creative thinking. Thinking, thinking, thinking. That is the nature of true science." On the final word he put a loud hissing sound.

"Shhh! Old Super-ears the Librarian is staring at you, Wardy."

"Sorry. I got carried away with all this thinking."

"I do have to admit Guterman's better than any of the teachers I had at the SL Center. And they're supposed to be the best."

"He's even semi-tamed the class clowns. Since that first day with the skeleton." Rolling up a magazine and using it like a microphone, he assumed the assertive tones of a news reporter. "Excuse me, Mr. Heinrich Guterman? The famous German exchange teacher from Evanstown High? Could you tell the viewing audience if you've ever had any slipups in your career as a famous scientist?"

"Why no, Herr Reporter," Wardy answered himself with an exaggerated accent. "Once I dispensed with the skeleton in my closet, my career just took off."

"Shhh," Meg whispered again. "She'll kick you out."

"Anyway, it's nice to have one class now where I don't have to worry about being Eaglebait."

"Wardy." Meg chewed her pencil in thought. "Have

you ever noticed how Mr. Guterman focuses on you—I mean a lot?"

He thought for a while. "I think you're right. Those eyes of his. They could burn a hole through a person. Baby-blue laser beams aimed right at me."

"Do you suppose he's trying to keep your attention on classwork, or do you think it's something more?"

"The man is forcing me to use my brain, that's all. I never thought I'd live to admit it, but biology is fun. Fascinating. I love it."

"I know. I've learned so much more from Mr. Guterman than I ever got out of Mr. Whitcomb's class." Her eyes widened. "We'd better get back to work. Super-ears is giving us the stink-eye again."

Finished with their library research at last, they stood outside the school building. It was one of those bright, cold winter afternoons when the sky looked summer blue, but the air pinched bare cheeks and noses. Wardy jammed his wool hat down over his ears and flipped up his coat collar. He turned to wave good-bye to Meg, who was standing on the curb waiting for her ride. "See y' tomorrow," he called. A sudden thought occurred to him; he turned and retraced his steps. "Hey," he puffed when he reached Meg's side. "Want to come to my house after school tomorrow? We can work on our project and…I could show you an experiment I've got going. It's in my basement lab. But it's a secret. You can't tell anybody about it."

Meg's warm brown eyes met his. "I guess so," she said in her soft voice. "I'll have to check with my mom. I'll ask her tonight. It's hard to resist a secret."

"Okay. Ride my bus home after school. Maybe your mother could pick you up afterwards."

"Where do you live?"

"Randall Street. In the Overbrook subdivision. You know where it is?"

She nodded. "I'll ask my mom. She'll probably be overjoyed. She always wants me to make more friends. I'll let you know tomorrow in Latin, okay?"

"Right! See y'." Turning, he began a quick jog toward home. Three miles in this weather was unendurable at a more moderate pace. He'd measured the distance on the new tracking watch Grandma Lou had given him at a little over three miles. He was getting used to jogging home almost every day—lately he'd been staying after school with Meg and missing his bus. Much to his surprise, he kind of enjoyed the exercise. It gave him time to think, too. About his laser. Mr. Guterman. Meg.

Meg. She's gorgeous. A goddess. And she likes me. Why did I invite her to see my laser? Am I just trying to impress her? What if I blow it? What if Leslie ruins everything? Or Mom? Oh Lord. Why did I do it? Please, God. Let everything be cool tomorrow. Please.

Leslie sat in front of the TV in the family room stuffing popcorn into her mouth. Without pulling her eyes away from the screen, she waved her hand in the direction of the kitchen and spoke. "Postcard from Dad on the kitchen table."

"Dad? Where's Dad that he's sending postcards?"

"Bermuda." Leslie hadn't unlatched her focus from the TV screen.

Bermuda. No wonder his dad had missed last weekend. What was he doing in Bermuda? Picking up the card from the table, he read it at a glance. It was addressed to both him and Leslie. A joint postcard from the father they hadn't even seen for two weeks. *That's real dedication between father and child.* He couldn't shake off his bitter thoughts. Ripping the postcard in half, he walked back into the family room. "Here's your half of the happy message. Touching, isn't it?"

"At least he thought to write to us," Leslie said piously. "It proves he's thinking about us even if he can't be with us."

"Oh, sure. He's frolicking on some pink beach with a bikini bunny just thinking and thinking about his children and wishing they could be there. Ha." It made him mad the way Leslie could ruin a good mood in record time. He headed down the stairs to his lab. *Leslie. Got to get rid of Leslie tomorrow. But how?* Puttering and tidying, he tried to think of what he would say to Meg when she saw the lab tomorrow. Should he act humble and dumb—or get right in and show her his stuff? Upstairs he heard the phone ring four, five times. Where was Leslie? Surely the sound of the phone would be enough to rouse her from her TV coma.

"Wardy! Wardy, phone's for you," she yelled down the stairs. Who would be calling him? Nobody ever called him. He locked up and went upstairs to answer the phone.

It was Grandma Lou. "Wardy, how are you?"

"Fine. Super. Things are going a little better here, Grandma Lou."

"Listen, this is a long distance call, so I'll have to hurry. I'm going to be in Evanstown tomorrow. Staying a couple of days."

"Hey, terrific. I can't wait to talk to you. There's so much…"

"Save it. Face-to-face is much better. How about

right after school? Can we go out for dinner or something? I thought I'd reserve a day for you and one for Leslie—so I can enjoy your company separately."

Tomorrow after school? Darn. What about his date with Meg? Wardy brightened. "Grandma Lou, would it matter too much if we switched it—if you and Leslie had your day tomorrow, and you and I went out the next day? It works better for me that way."

"Sure. No problem. We're on for day after tomorrow, then."

Wardy hung up. That would take care of his bratty sister. Good old Grandma Lou. He really couldn't wait to see her. If she only knew how timely her visit was.

****

It was a short walk to his house from the bus stop, but the winter wind had touched Meg's cheeks with pink, made her laugh more breathless than ever. Wardy's heart raced as he fumbled with the key in the lock to the front door. He hoped this wasn't all a terrible mistake.

"Would you like a snack before we get to work?" he asked.

"Sure. But I want to see the secret in the basement. Before we get to work on our project, I mean."

Opening the refrigerator, Wardy took out a bottle of milk. He pointed to the cabinet, and Meg got out two glasses. They sat on stools at the kitchen counter, drinking milk and helping themselves to cookies from the jar. Wardy couldn't taste a thing. He chewed and swallowed by reflex, surprised when he realized his glass was empty.

"I thought you had a younger sister," Meg said.

"I do. She's with Grandma Lou today."

"Grandma Lou?"

"Haven't I ever told you about my grandmother?"

"Only that you think a lot of her. Think she's understanding."

"She's the only person in my whole family who really cares about me. I wish you could meet her. You'd love her, too."

"I hope I will—meet her, that is. Someday." Meg stood up. "Now can we go see your experiment? I'm dying of curiosity."

She followed him down the stairs, peering this way and that, like people do when they're in a new place. Wardy ushered her into the inner sanctum of his lab.

"Wow!" she exclaimed. "Where'd you get all this stuff?"

"Oh, here and there. Some of it my dad left when he moved out. Some of it I've collected over the years. Borrowed that chemistry manual over there from my old military school. Only they don't know about it. You might call it their going-away gift to me when they kicked me out."

He was surprised to hear himself talking so blithely about his dismissal from Martin-Barrett. It wasn't so long ago that the memory had still burned painfully. But Meg was so easy to talk to, and she was the only other person who had ever been inside his lab.

"What's that?" She pointed to the latest remake of his laser. He'd left the mirrors resting on the worktable, but the glass tube was set up and ready. "Is this it—your secret experiment?" She bent to examine the glass tube more closely. "What is it?"

"It's a laser. Actually, the second incarnation. The first one I sort of blew up. I call her Big Vi."

"You named it?" She picked up one of the mirrors

and examined it. "I've read about lasers, but I've never actually seen one." Gently, she tapped the glass tube, then leaned over and peered inside it from one end. "You say you blew one up? You mean it works?"

Wardy nodded. She was a wonderful audience. He pointed to the patched holes in the walls.

"This is fantastic. I can't believe you've done all this in your basement, without any help."

"Well, Meg, I *have* had some help, actually." And, without thinking, he found himself telling her all about the letterhead letters and the response from Dr. Lowry. Almost before he realized it, he'd told her about everything, including the stationery from Quick-Print. Watching her face closely, he was a little nervous. What if she didn't like it? It was, after all, a lie, passing himself off as a professor. She wasn't the type to approve of lies. He was sure of that. Anxiously, he awaited her reaction.

Meg broke out in the only full-bodied laugh he'd ever heard from her. "Oh my gosh! It's unbelievable. Mr. Guterman would approve, for sure. Using your 'basic knowledge to expand your horizons. Creative thinking elevated to the highest power.' I love it! I wish I could tell somebody."

He wanted to hug her right then and there. Put his arms around her and tell her she was wonderful. But he didn't know how. Didn't know the correct steps in the process or how to begin.

"We'd better get to work on our project now," Meg said in a reluctant tone. Apparently she was unaware of his surging emotions. "I'll have to call my mother soon." They left the lab, and Meg waited until Wardy locked the door. "Thanks for showing me your secret. It makes me feel…special."

Special? Oh, boy. It's special to me, too. If you only knew how special. You're *what's special.*

Waving good-bye to Meg as her family car pulled away, Wardy felt a vibration from his phone in his pocket. A text. Now, who could be sending him a text? His grandmother always used the landline, and he'd just talked to her. It wouldn't be Grandma Lou. He knew Meg's parents hadn't allowed her to have a cell phone. He pressed the message button and read, then re-read the text: *Think u r smart Eaglebait? Stay tuned.* Instantly, another beep sounded. *Eaglebait is a dumbass!* Then another beep: *We hate Eaglebait, oh yeah!* If Wardy had overcome the Eaglebait brand in Mr. G's biology class, evidently, the message hadn't reached everybody at school.

Hastily, Wardy clicked the *end* button on his phone, shutting it down. First the Facebook page: *"Click if you find Eaglebait repulsive."* Pictures posted of skeletons named Eaglebait. Now a bunch of text messages all meant to bully him—make him feel lower than dirt. Technology: A wonder when it came to science but for slandering victims—not so wonderful.

Okay. So what? I've got a lot of good things going now. Plenty to keep me busy. And a new friend—a real friend. Grandma Lou would tell me to ignore the jerks doing this bullying. Easier said than done, but easier now that I've found a few people to support me—all because of science—of all things.

Chapter Eleven

The room was utterly silent. Mr. Guterman rose from his stool and swept the class with his oddly penetrating gaze. Wardy often wondered how he managed to connect one-on-one with thirty people at the same time.

"Meg, Wardy—that was an outstanding report. Outstanding. Particularly the documentation on experiments in other parts of the world. The diagram was enlightening and artistic as well. Thorough research. Excellent work." There was a rustling, murmuring sound in the classroom. People nodded, apparently agreeing with Guterman. Wardy couldn't believe it. To get the group's approval like that—he had never experienced it before. It gave him a dizzy feeling. Beside him, he could feel Meg glowing, basking in their shared praise.

The bell rang. No doubt about it—Wardy knew Meg would be waiting in the hall for him today. He collected his materials, jamming everything into a green garbage bag to carry home. Meg had already gone out, but she'd be waiting, he was sure. Pushing his chair under the table, he started to leave.

"Wardy? Could we talk for a minute?" It was Mr. Guterman's unmistakably modulated voice.

"Huh? Oh, sure." Wardy released the neck of the plastic bag, and it slumped limply to the floor.

"I have been observing you, Wardy," Mr. Guterman

began. He pronounced the *s* in *observing* like an *s, not a z.* "You have been my student for what—over a month now, correct?"

Wardy inclined his head, held by the teacher's clear, direct gaze.

"Do you remember the diagnostic test I gave out the first day? You were the last student to turn it in. We talked a bit afterward."

Again, Wardy nodded. What was Guterman getting at?

"I read your answers with special care. You see, even then, on the first day, I perceived that you were different."

Wardy winced.

Guterman seemed to pick up on Wardy's reflexive response. "Truly brilliant people are different. But it is a difference they can learn to value in themselves; ultimately, others will learn to do the same."

Wardy continued to stare into the ice-blue eyes. *What's he trying to say? My intelligence has caused my friendless life? Does he know what a klutz I am? How unattractive? How could I be "brilliant"? Brilliant people get straight A's, not straight D's. He's way off base.*

"I think today you're tasting the sweetness of academic accomplishment. In school, in front of your peers. It is an exhilarating feeling, yes?" Guterman's eyes were bright as marbles. "You can see the connection between hard work, intelligence, and rewards, yes?"

Mesmerized by the smoothness, the evenness of the voice, the riveting gaze, Wardy continued to stare mutely at his teacher.

"You realize that it may not be enough just being

smart—hiding your brilliance under your misfit mask. It is more pleasant to gain some recognition for the bright light of your mind. Let it illuminate the whole room. Finally, you are beginning to put some of your knowledge to use."

Praise. Mr. Guterman was handing out praise to *him,* Wardy Spinks, the joke of the school.

"That was an impressive report today. Critical thinking. That's what science, true science, is. Today you proved to me and to everyone in the class that you can do something with that mind of yours." As if for dramatic effect, Guterman paused. "It is a very exciting prospect. The application of creative genius to the technological betterment of mankind."

Genius. Genius? Does Guterman think I'm a genius? What if he's right? What if he's wrong? I've got to get out of here. Got to think.

"Go home now, Wardy. Think about today. Whenever you are ready, I will be ready to offer guidance. That's what teachers do best. They don't teach—they guide students into learning for themselves." Guterman pushed back from his desk and stood. "I am always in my office until five o'clock. Anytime you want to stay after for…for guidance, I will be there."

Still in a daze, Wardy made his way out into the hall. Meg tilted her head, curiosity raising her brows. "What was that all about? You and Guterman having a tete-a'-tete in there?"

Wardy stared at her blankly.

"Tete-a'-tete. You know, a head-to-head conversation."

Wardy shook his head. "I know what it means.

Sorry. My mind's on something else." He shook his head again. "He thought our report was brilliant. And—and he says I can stay after school for 'guidance' whenever I want to. You know, extra help and stuff, I guess."

Meg seemed disappointed. "Does that mean we won't be able to stay after school together?"

"Oh, no. It'd only be once in a while, I'm sure. How much time is a man like Guterman gonna devote to a kid like me?"

"Good. I'm glad. I want us to stay friends." *Yeah. Friends. Guterman didn't say one word about Meg's part in our "brilliant" report. Why did he give me all the credit? And why didn't I stick up for Meg's work?*

Meg began to walk, and Wardy fell in beside her. They strolled along the hall. Not many students hanging around, he noticed. Friday. The halls usually cleared out faster on Friday. They rounded the corner. Lounging against the wall in their familiar lethargic manner were the Marx Brothers—Jocko and Jimmo and the other two guys who'd pinned Wardy in the custodian's closet. Fear flickered inside him. Would they confront him while he was with Meg? Every step increased his apprehension. He wanted to turn and run; his instinct told him to clear out and quick, but with Meg beside him, he couldn't. He couldn't let her see what a coward he was. *Don't slow down and don't pay any attention to them.* Wardy swallowed; he could feel his Adam's apple bobbing like a cork on a fishing line.

They were oddly quiet, the Marx Brothers. None of their usual rowdiness, Wardy noticed. Thumbs hooked in their pockets, they just leaned on the lockers and watched but said nothing. *What's going on? Why don't they get on with it? Where's the joke for Eaglebait?*

Wardy made short work of exchanging books in his locker. Meg waited beside him. Could she sense his fear? He tried to hide his shaking fingers from her. Still no action from the jokers. *What are they going to do? When are they going to do it?*

He slammed his locker shut. "Let's go." He tried to keep the panic out of his voice. As they walked to the outside door, he couldn't resist a last glance at the four boys. He turned abruptly, wondering if they would try to follow.

"See y', Spinks," Jocko said. That was all. Just, "See y', Spinks." A strange feeling settled over Wardy. He was confused. Any other time, those guys would have leapt at the chance to show him up in front of a girl. What happened? Did it have anything to do with Guterman? Jocko and Jimmo, the smart half of the Marx Brothers, had been in his biology class when Guterman praised the report to the skies. Had Guterman cast a spell on them, too? He straightened his backpack over his shoulder. "Bye, Meg." He waved, setting off at a brisk pace. He'd think about it all as he ran home. And when he got there, he'd have worked out how he'd tell Grandma Lou. Grandma Lou was waiting.

****

Finally! Another email from Dr. Lowry. After quickly checking the message, he printed it, stuffed it into his pocket, and figured to read it later. Dropping his backpack on the bed, he grabbed a hairbrush and raked it through his tousled hair. In the mirror he noticed his color was up. His skin had lost the babyish white softness he'd always hated. All that jogging home from school, he supposed. Three miles, almost every day for a month. It was doing something to his weight, too. He hitched his pants to his waist. These days he could hardly keep them up—they'd become way too big for him. And he'd finally started growing taller again—at least an inch or two since he last measured.

"Wardy, taxi's here," Grandma Lou called up the stairs.

"Coming!" He dropped the brush, patted the print-out in his pocket, and charged out of the room. "Coming!" he called again.

"Where are we going?" he asked his grandmother as they settled into the backseat of the taxi.

"First, I have an errand to run at the mall, then I thought we'd get a bite at the health food restaurant there, if that's okay with you." She patted his knee. "It's a nice, quiet place to talk, and we need to catch up."

She spoke to the driver, and they headed for the main entrance to the mall.

"Where's your errand?" he asked conversationally.

"It's my glasses. I need some new frames. Seems you could use some new frames yourself."

She meant the taped part over his nose. "Yeah. A casualty of my last days at Martin-Barrett," he said.

"Have you ever considered contact lenses?" she asked. "Young as you are, they might improve your natural vision."

He shrugged. "Nope. Never thought about it."

"Well, while I'm at the optician's, why don't we see what the optometrist next door thinks. Dr. Lansing is an old crony of mine. If he's in, I'm sure he wouldn't mind checking your eyes."

An hour later they sat in the restaurant on the lower level of the mall. Wardy sipped his broccoli soup, trying to cool it off by blowing on the spoon. Grandma Lou was nursing a cup of hot spiced cider.

"Dr. Lansing says your lenses will be ready next week. He'll have to make sure they fit and give you instructions. Can you get your mother to take you back?"

"Guess so. She's been pretty busy selling real estate lately. We don't see much of her. I think it takes her mind off Dad and me and her other problems."

"Speaking of problems, how's it going with you and the school bullies?"

Reflectively, Wardy spooned his soup. "You know, some of the problems do seem to have thinned out for me. There's this girl named Meg Reilly, and she's beautiful. I mean *really* beautiful. She's my lab partner. And we got a new biology teacher, Heinrich Guterman. You know, he's the exchange teacher from Germany— the one I talked to early in the year about being a lab assistant. He's a terrific teacher. He thinks I'm brilliant. The other kids all like him—and the girls *love* him because he's so handsome. But he's going to help me with biology, maybe. And I've been thinking about showing him my experiments."

One after another, without much order, the words he'd stored up tumbled out, making Wardy sound like an excited two-year-old just learning to string ideas together.

Grandma Lou held up a protesting hand and laughed. "Wardy! Stop! I'm having trouble following all this. What do Meg Reilly and Heinrich Guterman have to do with your problems 'thinning out'?"

"I don't really know. That's the weird part. But the kids at school—you know, the ones who pick on me and play mean jokes—they've backed off. Slowed down. I don't know whether it's them or me. Or Meg or

Guterman. I tried to take your advice at Thanksgiving, you know. About ignoring the jerks who were making fun of me."

"So, do you feel—do you feel ignoring them worked?"

"I don't know. It helped, I think. I'm almost afraid to talk about it. Seems like the worst bullies—the Marx Brothers, as I call them—seems like they've backed off. I kind of feel like I can walk down the hall and not have to worry that somebody's going to dump water on my head or something. All I know for sure is, it began to get better when Mr. Guterman took over bio class." Pushing aside the empty soup bowl, he reached for his sandwich. "But…they did set up a Facebook page for people to post insults about me."

"Facebook?"

"Oh, I guess you don't know. . .or, do you know what Facebook is?"

"Surely you jest," she chuckled. "Why, I've had a Facebook Fan Page for a long time. My artist friends and critics like to post comments about my creations and events. Mostly complimentary, I'm happy to say and usually helpful."

"Yeah. Well, people who write on the *Eaglebait Facebook* page like to post comments about me. Nothing exactly complimentary or helpful, though."

Grandma Lou frowned slightly. "You've read these comments, I take it."

Wardy shrugged. "Enough to know the purpose is to bully me. Make me a laughingstock." He thought a minute. "But I haven't responded or anything. Just trying to follow your advice."

"I suspect that will eventually die a natural death,

then," she said. "One purpose of bullies is to get a rise out of their victims."

"But the texting is more of a problem," Wardy told her.

"Oh, I've had quite a learning curve with texting myself. My new iPhone—I wasn't about to let it get the best of me. So, I took an online course. I've become quite proficient with texting and apps and also with forwarding photos I take with my phone." She rummaged in her purse until she found the device, then showed it to Wardy. "I am even using it for phone calls!" She chuckled.

Wardy smiled. "Well, I guess I'm not surprised that you're a tech-y. But the texting problem I'm having is all about beep after beep telling me I'm a hopeless loser."

"I've heard about that kind of harassment. The electronic bully sends repeated insulting, rude messages."

"I've had to virtually shut down my new smartphone. Just when I was getting some great games and apps. Really makes me mad."

"Believe it or not, I've recently learned about a new app to counteract such messaging pranks. It's called 'Word Bully,' and it monitors your texts for specific bully-words and phrases—forwards them to a parent." She paused. "Or a grandparent. What do you think about that?"

Wardy retrieved his phone from his pocket and handed it over. "Go for it. Hope you're ready for some snarky vocabulary."

She smiled. "I'm quite sure I can handle it. I'll get this back to you as soon as possible. Now, tell me more about this Heinrich Guterman. You're talking to me, an old teacher, you know."

Taking a deep breath, Wardy launched into the events of the previous month, starting with the skeleton in Guterman's closet and winding up with the success of the biology report he and Meg had completed and the teacher's offer of further guidance.

Grandma Lou sat back from the table. "Well. Life has certainly taken a turn for you since Thanksgiving, I must say."

Wardy lowered his gaze, then faced his grandmother. "There's one more thing. I couldn't decide whether to tell you or not." He drew the printout from his pocket. "I got this e-mail today. It's from Dr. Robert Lowry in California. He's a physicist, and he…he thinks I'm one, too."

"Tell me more," Grandma Lou said. "I'd like to know all the details."

"I'll do better than that. We can read his e-mail together."

His grandmother said little after reading Dr. Lowry's e-mail. She paid the bill, and together they stood at the curb waiting for a taxi to take them home.

When she spoke, her tone was serious. "Of course, I'm disappointed in your falsehood. I think I understand why you felt you had to lie to the professor. Certainly, you've gotten some valuable free advice, but . . ."

"If it's any comfort, I *have* felt guilty. Every time I press 'send,' I feel a twinge."

The taxi arrived, and they climbed into the backseat, where they talked on in the dark.

"You have continued to write to Dr. Lowry, nevertheless. Under false pretense, correct?"

Wardy chose to ignore the question. "Did you see

what he said? He wants me to use a meter to measure the intensity and color of the light from my laser. The combination gives an accurate watt reading. Where would I get such a sophisticated instrument? I think I'm at the end of the road with Dr. Lowry anyway."

"Perhaps it's a good time to write and tell the good doctor the truth." His grandmother's voice was low and even.

"I'll think about it. Don't come down on me too hard, okay? For the first time in my life, things are beginning to make sense. For the first time I can remember in a long time, I'm happy to get up every day."

The taxi pulled into the driveway, and they got out. Walking up the front walkway, Wardy asked, "When will you be back again to visit?"

"My next exhibit will be in Washington, D.C."

"Wow! D.C.! Some glitzy galleries in the city, huh?"

She laughed. "That's the exact term Vanessa, my agent, uses. *Glitzy.* I expect it'll be exciting and maybe a bit scary. Anyway, I can't wait."

"I'm really happy for you," Wardy told her. "Happy you are so happy."

"And I am happy for *you,* dear grandson. Especially about Meg Reilly. She sounds like someone worth hanging on to."

Worth hanging on to. Worth standing up for? Why did I allow Guterman to leave Meg out? Give me all the praise? Will Meg want to stick around if she knows what a wimp I am?

Chapter Twelve

"You want me to be a lab assistant? For your physics class?" Wardy was incredulous. "But how?"

"I have already filled the chemistry lab job, but physics—well, I am very particular about my physics lab. You are to be my student lab assistant for the rest of the school year. It will work very well. I have checked with Miss Dawson in Guidance, and you will be allowed to drop Latin, which coincides with my physics class, at semester break." Guterman made it sound so simple. Wardy had been trying to get Miss Dawson to let him drop Latin since October; Guterman walks in off the street, so to speak, and charms her into it in a minute. Everybody was in awe of Guterman—even Miss Know-It-All Dawson in Guidance.

"But I've never taken any physics classes," Wardy said, still doubtful. "They're all upperclassmen in there, aren't they?"

Guterman scrutinized Wardy's face. "That is precisely what makes the arrangement so ideal. It eliminates the necessity for competition for the position within the class, allowing students to concentrate on their studies. At the same time, it provides a wonderful opportunity for you. An opportunity that may lead to future possibilities of enormous magnitude." Mr. Guterman never blinked once, Wardy realized, as the polysyllabic words slid off his cultivated tongue. Pearls of wisdom. Now Wardy knew how the phrase must have been coined—round, perfect beads of sound rolling out into the air.

"But…but how would I prepare? For experiments and things? I mean, I haven't been in physics class all year learning the principles like the rest of the people in there." Wardy heard the last bell ring. Another three-mile jog home today.

"I have done a thorough analysis of the situation. Believe me, you already know more principles of physics than you realize. The diagnostic told me that." Mr. Guterman's voice was so persuasive, almost hypnotic. Wardy could feel himself being swayed, even though the gnawing edges of insecurity bubbled underneath. "I'll need a knowledgeable, malleable lab assistant from outside—someone who loves science. You told me that once, you know. In our first interview."

Wardy gulped. How could he forget? He'd felt so foolish after he blurted it out in Mr. Guterman's tiny office that day. To think that the teacher had remembered his words. The man was an enigma. Wardy's eyes began to itch and water. His new contact lenses always gave him trouble after six hours or so. He needed to get them out, rest his eyes. He averted his gaze, but his resistance was ebbing. Mr. Guterman seemed completely set on the idea. And, what did he mean about "future possibilities of enormous magnitude"? Guterman was like a poker player: He never laid all his cards on the table, never let his expression reveal his hand. Wardy blinked and rubbed his eyes. "Okay. I guess so. If you think I can handle it, I'm willing to try."

"Such arrangements are frequently made in Europe. Teachers are encouraged to use the most qualified candidates for lab assistants—not necessarily the most convenient." Mr. Guterman's eyes held Wardy's. "As I remember, you once told me you've done many experiments on your own—in your personal lab. Would any of them involve physics, by any chance?"

" I—I'm working on a laser, actually. And fuels," Wardy stammered. Where had the words come from? He had not intended to mention his laser experiments to Guterman—not yet. But there it was—he'd told him. Wardy clamped his lips shut.

"Have you had any success with your laser experiments?"

"Some, I guess. Right now I'm trying to get an accurate reading on the watt power."

"How?"

"I'm using a photocell."

"But you find it a primitive instrument? You think you are in need of a more sophisticated instrument for accurate readings, yes?"

Wardy nodded. Guterman wasted no time in getting to the heart of the matter.

"Would you like to come over and see it?" There he went again. He had definitely not intended to extend an invitation. It was as though a ventriloquist had made the words come from his lips—pulled a string while he mouthed the sounds. Again, Wardy clamped his lips together. If he kept them firmly shut, no ventriloquist could make a dummy out of him.

"I would consider it an honor to come see your laser experiment." For the first time, a tiny smile played around the teacher's thin, firm lips. "When may I come?"

Wardy's pulse began to race. Why was he having such an attack of nerves? Was he afraid of being judged by Mr. Guterman? "Anytime…. How about…Friday?"

"Friday will be fine. We'll go after our lab session. We will need to conduct lab sessions in my office every day after school until you are ready to go into the physics lab. I am sure you understand the necessity for such preparation?"

Every day? Oh, boy. This is going to be intensive. Every afternoon studying physics with Mr. Guterman. Wow.

"We'll begin right now. Get your things. We're going to my office. We've a good hour of work ahead of us." Mr. Guterman stood up, collecting his briefcase and coat. "Follow me."

In the hall, Meg waited for him. She'd been there a long time, Wardy realized. Giving her a half-pleading shrug, he hurried after the brisk-paced Guterman. "I'll call you tonight," he mouthed to her. She gave him a weak wave before he rounded the corner out of sight.

****

His mother had invited Mr. Guterman to stay for dinner. Wardy wished fervently that she hadn't, but, since the teacher had already accepted, it was too late to do anything about it. Why did she have to be home from work today of all days?

Wardy was tired. It had been his first day in physics lab with the upperclassmen, and his nerves were shot. Everything had rolled right along, smooth as glass; Guterman had been a good coach during his after-school sessions. But reading the reactions of the other students in the lab was hard. If the students weren't friendly, at least they had appeared tolerant. Wardy gave Guterman credit for that. The man was a magician; he hypnotized everybody, ready to do his bidding.

The magic was working on his mother right now. She laughed in what Wardy referred to as her "real estate" voice. It was tinkly and merry and false. *Guterman's probably the best-looking guy Mom's seen in a long time.* Another peal of laughter broke forth from her.

"Take your time in Wardy's little workroom," his mother said to Mr. Guterman. "I'm going into the kitchen to whip up some dinner. A bit of home-cooked food for the hard-working scientists." Wardy cringed at her word choice—her tone.

Impatiently, Wardy shifted his weight from side to side. He wanted to get down to his workroom and get it over with. A knot of hope and dread, like a huge ball of ice, clutched his gut and threatened to freeze him from the inside out.

Shut up, Mom, will you? Just clamp it. Let's get going. Will I be a success or a failure in the master's eyes?

At last, they were inside the lab. Guterman was very quiet. He took a long time examining the laser. At one point he turned to Wardy, raising his eyebrows, asking silent permission to touch the equipment. Afraid to break the spell, Wardy nodded, giving the asked-for permission as wordlessly as it had been requested. The teacher went over every square inch of Wardy's laser, his face a study in concentration. At last, his expression relaxed, and he spoke for the first time.

"Excellent. Excellent. I knew I had chosen correctly." Mr. Guterman's features smoothed into a dazzling smile. The knot of ice melted in Wardy's stomach. Warm rivers of relief flowed through him. He had passed the test. They spent the next thirty minutes in a question-and-answer session. As he locked up the lab and led the teacher up the steps, Wardy still felt the warm glow of success.

They ate in the dining room, using linen napkins and sterling silver and the best China. The table was beautiful, with candles and a flower arrangement for the centerpiece. His mother had outdone herself with the meal, as well. They hadn't had a dinner like this for months, not since Dad left. Steak, a Caesar salad, and chocolate mousse for dessert. Mr. Guterman and his mother drank red wine with their meal. After a couple of glasses, his mother's eyes began to twinkle, and she started to flirt coquettishly with the teacher. If Mr. Guterman noticed, he covered it well with his famous poker face. He was charming and urbane, and seemed to be enjoying himself. Even Leslie was affected by his gracious manner—she was subdued and polite in a way Wardy had never seen before.

Long after the finish of the meal, they sat at the table talking. "Now I think I must go, Mrs. Spinks," Mr. Guterman finally said. "Thank you for a delightful meal and charming company."

"Oh, do call me Gwen. I hope you'll come as often as you like. I'm sure Wardy would enjoy your help."

Wardy stiffened.

"Wardy seems to have accomplished a great deal on his own," Mr. Guterman said smoothly. "He really is quite intelligent, Mrs. Spinks—Gwen. In fact, I hope you will consider allowing Wardy to attend our Summer Youth Institute of Science in Germany after school is over this year."

Wardy stared at the teacher with his mouth open. What was this?

"Of course, he will have to do intense preparation between now and June in order to be ready. Not many American students are invited, you see. It is considered quite an honor."

Is this what Guterman had meant when he'd talked about "future possibilities of enormous magnitude"?

His mother was completely taken. She broke out in a wide smile. "It sounds like a wonderful experience for Wardy," she gushed. "Would you really be willing to do all that for my son?"

"It would be a credit to me if he should come to the institute. Wardy has a fine scientific mind—a mind that will be put to use at the institute. But he will have to be willing to work hard—very hard—to qualify." His teacher rose from the table. "Perhaps we can discuss the details another time?"

"Of course," Gwen answered quickly. Too quickly. "Why don't you come to dinner one day next week— Friday perhaps—and we'll talk more about Wardy's going to Germany for the summer." She extended her hand to the teacher. "Thank you for being such a charming guest, Mr. Guterman."

"Heinrich," he said. "Please call me Heinrich, Gwen."

****

"Hey, Meg. It's me—Wardy. Sorry to call you so late. I didn't wake you up, did I? Mr. Guterman just left. I showed him the laser." Even though he was in his room with the door closed, he lowered his voice almost to a whisper so his mother wouldn't know he was making such a late phone call.

"I thought you said it was a secret, Wardy. You told me not to tell anybody." Meg's soft voice held an accusing note.

"I really didn't mean for him to see it. Not yet, anyway. It just kind of happened. Then my mom invited him for dinner, and he stayed late."

"We never see each other anymore. You're not even in Latin class now."

"I know. And Guterman keeps me after school working on physics labs every day. But it's only a temporary arrangement with Guterman, I'm sure, and — and we're still lab partners. We get to sit together in biology."

"I get the feeling Guterman would change that, too, if he could," Meg said ruefully.

"What do you mean?" Wardy was puzzled.

"Maybe I'm imagining things, but it just seems Guterman's trying to keep us from, well, from *being* together, or something. Maybe I got spoiled having our talks after school. Now you have to dash off to Guterman's office every day." She paused. "First, he gets you out of Latin. Then he breaks up our after-school time . . ."

Wardy gave a short laugh. "That can't be true. It only seems that way. Why would Guterman want to do a thing like that? Break up our friendship, I mean?"

There was a short silence. "Well, you're probably right. I miss you, though. Talking. Working on projects. It was fun." Her whispery voice rustled over the phone, sending shivers through Wardy.

Hurriedly, he changed the subject, hoping to distract Meg from her concerns. "You should see what I'm learning in our afternoon sessions. 'Tutorials,' Guterman calls them. Fascinating, exciting stuff. Very advanced, some of it—so many experiments I've only dreamed about. I love physics. It's really my bag. And guess what? Guterman's invited me to spend the summer in Germany to attend some science institute for youth. He says it's a real honor to be invited."

"See. He's even planning to separate us for the summer." Meg sighed, exhaling loud enough for Wardy to hear. "Just kidding. I'm really very happy for you. It sounds like a great opportunity." She paused. "Don't let it go to your head, now that you're getting slim and tall. No more glasses, even. Seems there's less gossip about that Eaglebait nonsense."

Wardy gave a self-conscious laugh. "Do you think I've improved? You're the only one I care about...noticing how I...how I might have changed, I mean."

"Fishing for compliments, Wardy? I always liked you for your mind. Who could ask for a better lab partner?"

For a long time they talked. Conversation with Meg Reilly was so easy now that they'd broken the silence barrier. She wasn't the only one who missed their after-school time together. He'd like to have a real date with Meg some time. Alone. The thought made his heart pound. Should he ask her out? What if she said no? Would his asking alter their wonderful, delicate friendship? He had no idea how to bring up the subject—he'd never been interested in a girl before. Meg was on another topic now, and the opportunity passed. Finally they finished talking and hung up. It was after eleven o'clock—late enough—but Wardy was hardly sleepy. He was filled with adrenaline—charged up. No way would he get to sleep. He stepped into his room and locked the door. Pulling up his email screen, he began his letter.

Dear Dr. Lowry. I hope you'll understand everything I've done when you finish reading this e-mail and know I never meant any harm. My name is Ward M. Spinks, Jr., but I'm called Wardy, and I'm not a physicist. I'm not anything. I'm a freshman at Evanstown High School, and I built a laser in my basement... On and on he wrote, explaining everything. He signed it "Wardy." With a sigh, he re-read the message and then pressed *send*, before he could change his mind.

I did it, Grandma Lou. Told him the truth. Now I'll probably never hear from him again. But there's no turning back now. The truth is out.

He climbed into bed and lay for a long time mulling over the day's events. As he drifted into sleep, a thought occurred to him. *I didn't tell Guterman about Dr. Lowry. Purposely didn't tell him. I wonder if I should?*

Chapter Thirteen

The hall phone rang again. Wardy locked his workroom door and hurried up the basement stairs to answer it. Where was Leslie? Why didn't she answer the phone? All she ever did was sit in front of the television and stuff her face. He had important things to do with his time—and more and more demands were being made on it every day.

"Hello?" he said breathlessly.

"Wardy? This is Eric Sanderson. You sound out of breath."

"Yeah. Ran up the stairs to answer the phone."

"Sorry. I don't have your cell number. Hey, me and two other guys in biology class—Chuck Shapiro and Bob Raiford—we were wondering if you wanted to go in on a project with us for science fair."

"Science fair? When is it?"

"Not until April—that gives us a couple of months. We want to do something big. Biophysics, maybe. We thought . . ."

"You thought I ought to know something about physics by now, right?" Wardy gave a short laugh.

"Yeah. Something like that. There's a big cash prize for the winning district this year—we want to go for it."

Wardy hesitated. He was so busy already with Guterman after school every day. And now he was doing a lot of homework to try to get the rest of his grades up.

And spending every other weekend with Dad. It didn't leave much time to work on the laser. But April sounded like a long way off.

"What kind of project did you guys have in mind?" Wardy stalled for time.

"That's where you come in. We thought you might have some bright ideas. We meet tomorrow night at my house. Seven o'clock. We'll send out for pizza, so don't eat before you come. What d'y' think?"

It had been a long time since anybody had invited Wardy to do anything. "Okay, fine. See you tomorrow night."

"Good. I'll give you directions to my house in class tomorrow. See y'."

Wardy hung up the phone thoughtfully. Eric and Chuck and Bob—they were okay guys. Not the practical-joker types. He used to lump all the Evanstown kids into one big adversary: them against him, Eaglebait. Now he was beginning to realize differences among people. Big differences. There were some okay kids at school after all. Plus, if Eric didn't have Wardy's cell number, he couldn't be involved in sending any of those nasty texts he'd been getting.

It made him think of Meg. A good time to call her. He hadn't talked to her in a couple of days—not really. You couldn't count the talk they did as lab partners. He missed their casual after-school conversations. In the back of his mind, he still hoped to get up the nerve to ask her for a date. Picking up his cell phone, he pulled up her contact info and pressed "call," but there was no answer. Well, he really didn't have time to talk anyway. He still had a big English paper due, and he hadn't even started. As usual, he'd become involved with Big Vi and lost track of time.

Entering his room, he paused before the full-length mirror hanging on the closet door. There really had been some physical changes in the past months. His new height made the weight-loss more dramatic. He turned sideways and checked over his shoulder. Yep. You could almost say he was tall and slim. No more pudgy baby fat. And, minus the glasses, his face appeared better, too—with the addition of a little ruddy color, from all the jogging in the winter wind. Straightening his shoulders and sucking in his gut like they'd had to do at MBA, he laughed out loud and made a sudden grab for his belt. His pants had almost fallen off! He'd have to talk somebody into getting him some new clothes—taller, slimmer clothes. Maybe Dad. It would keep him from having to talk to Wardy if they spent a few weekends shopping for clothes. Dad would like that—not having to talk.

Sitting down at his desk, he adjusted the lamp and sorted through his books and papers, trying all the while to think up a good dramatic topic for his creative writing assignment for English class. Suddenly, he had it. He'd write a short story about a budding young scientist in a military school who set out to make nitroglycerin in the chemistry lab after hours. Only he got caught, kicked out, sent home. Wardy bent to his task.

Mr. Guterman made it all sound so natural. It wasn't until later that Wardy realized Meg had predicted this would happen. Since Eric and Wardy had decided to do a science fair project together, Guterman said it was logical they should be lab partners. So, Guterman switched Meg to Eric's table to be partners with Mary Anne Souder and Eric to sit at Wardy's table. Chuck and

Bob were already lab partners, so it all made perfect sense, according to Guterman. They were going to work on amino acids, they'd decided at Chuck's house, and now they could use class time to work on the project. The only thing was, there'd be no more Meg Reilly beside him at the lab table every day. No more sweet, soft, quiet Meg.

He gathered his books together, ready to go to Guterman's office for his tutorial. About half their sessions now were spent on what the teacher referred to as "prepping" for the Summer Youth Institute of Science. Lots of laser technology, which Guterman said was the number-one topic for the coming summer session. Leaving the classroom, Wardy turned down the hall to Guterman's office. Meg stood in his path.

"Meg! Were you waiting for me? I've got to go work with Guterman again today." He talked rapidly; he was already late, and Guterman disapproved of tardiness. Seeing her standing in the hall alone, with the late afternoon sun glinting on her soft hair, he felt all the old emotions rush back—like waves splashing onto a sunny shore. He wished he could stop to talk. Be with her. Walk down the hall in a leisurely fashion enjoying their time together. But it was impossible. Guterman was expecting him.

Meg gazed at him solemnly and handed him a folded sheet of notebook paper. "I told you Guterman was trying to separate us. Don't let him, Wardy. Don't let him dominate you all the time." Turning, she ran down the hall, but Wardy rushed after her, caught her arm, and pulled her around to face him.

"What do you mean? What are you talking about, Meg? Are you crazy?"

Tears glistened at the corners of her eyes. "Read the note, Wardy," she choked. "Just read it." Turning again, she fled.

Dumbfounded, Wardy stood in the hall and tried to think. Why was she so upset? She was exaggerating everything. So—they were no longer lab partners sitting together at the same table—was that important enough to Meg to generate tears? He turned to go back to Mr. Guterman's office. "Don't let Guterman dominate you." *Dominate? Is that what he does—dominate me?*

Carefully, he placed the note inside his wallet and slipped it into his back pocket. No time to read now. Later—after he got home. Then he'd call Meg. Talk it all out, tell her she was overreacting. He picked up his pace. He was very late for his tutorial.

The teacher's back greeted him as he thrust open the door and dropped his backpack on the side table. Mr. Guterman had managed to fill every available corner of the tiny office. Beside his desk and Wardy's chair, a metal filing cabinet and shelves of books and equipment stretched from floor to ceiling. Mr. Guterman was filing some folders in the cabinet, but he turned as Wardy dropped his backpack.

"Sorry I'm late. I needed to…to talk to someone."

"It is all right. I had to do some filing before we start today." Guterman's even, clipped voice showed no impatience with his tardiness to Wardy's relief. "Is it Meg Reilly? She is upset about the new lab partner, yes?" The *s* hissed at the end of his question.

Startled at his teacher's perception, Wardy blinked and nodded.

"Yes. I thought so. I could see it in her eyes. She thinks a lot of you. I believe. Females. They get involved emotionally and fail to sort out the important from the unimportant. Science must always come first for the truly dedicated scientist."

What was Guterman's point? Why was he saying this now?

"Women can be useful, of course, but they must not be allowed to step out of line when there is important—crucial—work to be accomplished. Technology cannot wait for sentimentality. She must understand that."

Wardy did not know what to think. He knew Guterman was drawing a stereotype he himself did not agree with or approve of, but he wasn't sure why the teacher was bringing up the subject now. He certainly didn't want any part of something that would hurt Meg, but Guterman made it sound like there were only two choices, science or love. The flip side to the coin—take your choice. And hadn't Guterman been friendly enough with his mother? All at once, he felt stifled in this tiny room with Mr. Guterman's overwhelming presence. He could not think clearly about his feelings for Meg here. He was only getting more mixed up. Had Meg been right? *Dominate? Or is it permeate? Guterman seeps through my pores, engulfs my thoughts.*

Wardy tried to shake off the feeling. If Meg was being overly emotional, he couldn't let it affect him now. There was work to be done. Time was fleeting. Pulling his chair closer to the teacher's desk, he cleared his throat and asked, "Where do we begin today?"

****

Gwen shook her head and frowned. She talked half to herself, half to Wardy. "I'm late, and Heinrich is coming to take me out to dinner tonight, but I have an important business call to make first." She began dialing hurriedly. "Heinrich is so punctual. Must be a German trait."

Wardy shut the door to his room and felt for the smartphone in his pocket. Now that Grandma Lou and her Bully Word app blocked the nasty text messages, he enjoyed using it again. Though her phone rang and rang, there was no answer at Meg's house. It wasn't likely he'd get a chance to call again after he got to Dad's apartment. Dad liked to keep Leslie and him running here and there all the time. And there were always mobs of people milling around at Dad's—no privacy at all.

He really needed to talk to Meg. He had read her note, evidently, scribbled hastily in biology class after Guterman moved her. It was somewhat incoherent, but the gist of it was that she was beginning to feel very uneasy about his relationship with Guterman. *"I've got a feeling he's using you,"* she'd written. *"For what, I don't know, can't imagine. But it scares me. You're spending more and more time under him, Wardy.* Under. *He's dominating your life."* He had to talk to Meg—tell her that her imagination was going overboard. *"I like you, Wardy,"* she'd ended the note. *"I feel like you're a true friend. But I feel Guterman's afraid of that—of our friendship. I can sense his fear, and it scares me."* She signed it *"Love, Meg."* Love. Who was right? Meg or Guterman? The flip side of the coin again. You had to choose one or the other; you couldn't have both. Why not?

A car engine rumbled in the driveway. Dad already? No. There was no familiar honking. It was Guterman—Heinrich—come to pick up Wardy's mother for their dinner date. Involuntarily, Wardy grimaced. He didn't approve of this relationship between Guterman and his mother. He knew she was quite taken with the handsome German, but Mr. Guterman didn't seem the type for a romantic relationship. All that talk about science coming first. His mother's "real estate" laugh made him scowl. "I wish she wouldn't do that," he muttered under his breath.

"I'm almost ready, Heinrich. Just let me lock the back door and get my purse." Her voice trailed off as they moved farther away from the foyer. Wardy picked up his phone again. He simply had to get hold of Meg. Then his mother's simpering laugh sounded closer as they moved in the direction of the foyer below him. Wardy couldn't resist eavesdropping on their conversation.

"I think it's wonderful, Heinrich, what you've done for Wardy." He couldn't hear the reply, though he strained his ears hard and moved closer to the top of the stairs. His mother's voice rang out like a church bell. "Why, you've become the mentor I'd always hoped Wardy would find. A real mentor. You've taken him under your wing and brought out all the good qualities I always knew he had hidden deep inside. He was a lost soul until you came to Evanstown High and rescued him. Now he's blossomed into a red-blooded, American kid. And we owe it all to you."

Red-blooded American kid? Is that what she's always wanted? Why didn't she say so—save us all a lot of grief.

Wardy could hear their talk clearly now—both of them. Cautiously, he stepped back inside the door to his room so the two wouldn't see him.

His mother continued, "Why, do you know what they call Wardy? Leslie told me they wrote it all over the school. Wardy Spinks is—"

"Eaglebait," Mr. Guterman said in his low, even, modulated voice. "Wardy Spinks is Eaglebait."

Chapter Fourteen

Dear Dr. Lowry:

Thanks for writing back to me. I was afraid you wouldn't ever want to again after you found out I'm not really a scientist—yet. But the advice you gave me in your letters has helped a lot with my laser. It kept me from making stupid mistakes and encouraged me to continue working. Most of all, though, I think it's great that you've asked me to keep writing to you now that you know I'm only a kid who loves physics and chemistry.

Since I first wrote to you, something really cool has happened. An exchange teacher from Germany, Heinrich Guterman, came to take my biology teacher's place. Mr. Guterman is a very smart physicist, and he's taught me so much. He made me his lab assistant in physics class, and every day after school he tutors me. He's seen my laser, too, and he said he was impressed. Mr. Guterman invited me to attend the Summer Youth Institute for gifted science students. It's in Germany this summer, and he's been preparing me for participation in the institute. He says I am his protege.

I think you'd be interested in the stuff Mr. Guterman's teaching me—it's all about laser technology as it's applied to defense systems. I'm learning about orbiting "death rays" that can obliterate intercontinental missiles. They could make nuclear missiles obsolete, Mr. Guterman says. He thinks they could save the world from the catastrophe of nuclear winter that might result from massive nuclear war. "The technological betterment of mankind," Mr. G. calls it.

I get the feeling he'd like for me to "go public" with my laser, but I'm not ready yet. It's a little hard to explain, and I'm not completely sure I understand it myself. I know the laser's not perfect, but that's not what's bothering me. Sorry, I'm being too vague—I know that.

I want to keep writing to you, Dr. Lowry. You were the first person to take me and my science seriously. I'll let you know how my experiments are going, too. Thanks again.

Wardy read and re-read his message before pressing *send* and closing his laptop. He had hidden himself away in the small study of his father's apartment to get away from the noise—to think and write to Dr. Lowry. Dad always had swarms of people in and out of his apartment on weekends playing music, dancing, eating, and drinking. It gave Wardy a headache. Right now he needed to collect his thoughts on a lot of things, but Dad's apartment was not the place for reflective thinking.

Would Dr. Lowry understand his reluctance to bring Big Vi out of the basement? Was he being foolish? Wardy wished he could talk to Meg about the idea. Mr. Guterman had been hinting pretty broadly about getting the laser ready for display.

Meg. He wanted to hear her voice—to talk and talk, like old times. Was he being soft—foolish—like Guterman seemed to think? He'd tried to call her, but there was no answer. Probably she was out to dinner with her family. He remembered Meg had once told him they usually went out to eat on weekends. Maybe, while he was in the quiet little room here, he would try to write her a note. Taking out a fresh piece of paper, he began.

Draft after draft ended up crumpled and tossed into the trash can. Why couldn't he get down on paper what he wanted to say—what he had to say? Why was it so difficult? At long last he sat re-reading the short note. It still was not right, but it seemed to be the best he could do.

Dear Meg,

I've been trying to call you but haven't gotten through. Maybe it's better this way. I really like you, Meg. You're the only friend I had at Evanstown High for a long time. I love talking to you, being with you. But I'm involved in some really big deals now. Guterman says science is more important than everything else—even friendships. Right now my time is all taken up with science. I have to get ready for the Summer Youth Institute. I have to prepare for physics lab. Eric and Chuck and Bob and I have to work on our science fair project. And, then, there's my laser. So, I guess there's no time left for anything else.

But I want to stay friends. When I get done with all this work, I hope we'll be able to spend time together like we used to. If you still care, I mean.

I'll see you in bio class.

Love,

Wardy

P.S. I wrote to Dr. Lowry and told him the truth.

P.P.S. I still think you're beautiful.

Mr. Guterman would not approve of the second postscript, but Wardy left it in the final letter anyway. He wasn't sure why, but it seemed important. He planned to give Meg the note in biology on Monday. He'd made the decision—written the letter—but he felt oddly unrelieved. The whole business left him with a bad taste in his mouth and a throbbing headache. *It must be the atmosphere here at Dad's. Too much stale smoke, too many dishes littered about. I need a breath of fresh air. It's depressing. All of it.*

Leaving the study, he wound his way out to the balcony, where he stood inhaling deeply in the cold night air. But his headache pulsed on like an old bruise, spreading under the skin of his forehead. And he couldn't shake the empty, deflated feeling—the sense of loss that went with his note to Meg.

****

Grandma Lou's eyes lit up like Fourth of July sparklers. "Gwen, I tell you, the exhibit opening was wonderful! You should see the gatherings these people put on. All the men in black tie and the women wearing the most exotic gowns, jewels, and furs— uniformed waiters handling trays of appetizers and drinks, known dignitaries mingling with the crowd. It's simply dazzling! I've always heard that an opening in Washington is exhilarating, and now I know why. The people, the attention—I felt so…so appreciated. I even forgot to be nervous after the first few minutes." Gwen listened to her mother's ecstatic monologue with more indulgence than Wardy had seen her display in a long time. She was willing to tolerate others' needs once her own had been well met, he realized with a jolt. At the moment, Heinrich Guterman seemed to have supplied his mother with all she required for personal fulfillment.

The change had not gone unnoticed by Grandma Lou. "Why, Gwen, you seem so relaxed and happy.

Things must be going well for you these days."

"Believe it or not, Wardy is the one responsible for my current happy state," Gwen told her mother. "His new teacher—Heinrich Guterman—you know—we've been—well, seeing each other—seeing quite a lot of each other."

"It certainly seems to have done you a world of good." Grandma Lou arched her eyebrows and rolled her eyes toward Wardy. "But how does Ward, Jr. feel about this new relationship?"

Gwen smiled, but her voice held an edge. "It's out of Wardy's hands now, Mom. Heinrich's wining and dining me on a regular basis. These Europeans certainly know how to pamper a girl. Tonight, he's taking me dancing. Now I have to get ready."

Wardy wanted to throw up. Why he reacted so violently to his mother's going out with Mr. Guterman, he wasn't sure. But nauseated was a mild way of describing how he felt. Horribly disgusted, irretrievably mortified would be closer to the truth. Why would a guy like Guterman be interested in his mother?

Grandma Lou drew Wardy to her side. Because he'd grown taller, she had to stand on tiptoe to whisper in his ear. "Come to the kitchen. We'll be able to talk there."

Gwen turned to leave. "Stick around, Mom. You can meet Heinrich when he comes to pick me up tonight."

"I'd like nothing better." Grandma Lou and Wardy ambled into the kitchen.

"Tell me more about your show," Wardy said, sitting down across the table from her.

"Oh, this is a fine life for me. I feel I've finally come of age. So many artists are never recognized until after they're dead and gone." She stood up to prepare herself a cup of tea. "Do you want anything to drink?"

"No, thanks."

She popped a tea mug into the microwave. "Now," she said, sitting down again with the hot mug, "tell me what's been going on in *your* life. I swear, you're getting to be so mature; you're quite grown-up. Next thing you know, you won't want to tell your old grandmother anything at all."

Wardy gave her a reassuring smile. "I doubt that. You're my sounding board. Always have been."

She patted his hand. "Well, out with it. What's up?"

"I'm really involved with a lot of new projects. Mr. Guterman's keeping me busy as his lab assistant—physics lab, can you believe it? And he's teaching me laser technology and getting me ready for the Summer Youth Institute, and . . ."

"Wow! Slow down and let me get a handle on all this." His grandmother laughed. "Now, start over. Lab assistant. What you're learning and what your duties involve. All the details. One at a time."

It was a long recital. He hadn't meant to tell Grandma Lou about the note he'd written Meg, but in her quiet way, she got it out of him. "And what was Meg's reaction to this note?" she asked.

Perplexed for a moment, he didn't say anything, then he spoke out hurriedly, "She hasn't spoken to me since I gave it to her. Not a word."

"Not a word?"

"I catch her eying me in class sometimes, but she refuses to talk to me in class anymore. She actually turns her back to me if I try to say something to her. I guess I blew it. I wanted us to stay friends."

"So, in class, her expression is…?"

"Scared—a combination of scared and sad. Like she might start to cry or something."

For a long moment, his grandmother observed him. "You feel you made the right choice, then. With Meg?"

"At the time it seemed right. Now—I'm not so sure. I miss her more than I ever thought I would. It's not like she's my only friend anymore, like it was at first. I mean, Eric and Chuck and Bob—we do things together, mostly work on our science fair project. But sometimes we grab a pizza or do something fun if we finish up early. And other kids at school—seems like they're friendlier now. Some speak to me in the halls. Some of the girls, too. Lisa Wilson's having a party next weekend, and she invited me." He stopped and shook his head. "But with Meg acting like this, I feel lonely, like there's a big part of my life missing. "

"I think your Meg Reilly must be a very genuine person. Very genuine and very sensitive. Maybe she expects more from you than you do from yourself."

"But Mr. Guterman—he's . . .he's giving me so much. It's a rare opportunity. I don't know if I can afford to screw up anything."

"Does Mr. Guterman make you feel that way—that you might jeopardize the plans he has for you if you keep your friendship with Meg?"

Wardy shook his head again. "Yes—no—in a way. Oh, I don't know. I'm really mixed up. He doesn't seem to like Meg, for some reason. He doesn't come right out and say it, of course, but he makes me *feel* I shouldn't spend any time with her. When I'm with Mr. Guterman, I think I know what's right, but when I get away from him and try to think—well, it all comes out different."

The front doorbell rang. Wardy jumped. "There he

is—Mr. Guterman, here to get Mom. Come on. You've got to meet him."

Setting down her tea mug, she laughed good naturedly. "My goodness. Everyone's so set on my meeting this gentleman. He must be something indeed."

Gwen rushed to open the front door as Wardy and Grandma Lou walked into the foyer. Mr. Guterman stepped through the door, stunningly handsome in a dark three-piece suit—European cut, of course. His blond hair was perfectly styled and his square jaw cleanly shaven.

"Wardy's grandmother," he exclaimed warmly when introduced. He took her hand and bowed over it elegantly. "I am delighted to meet you. I have heard many wonderful things about you."

"Thank you, Mr. Guterman. I've been hearing a lot about you, too." She put her arm around Wardy. "I think it's wonderful the way you're encouraging my grandson's scientific leanings. You could have a distinct impact on his future, you know."

Gwen kissed her mother lightly on the cheek. "See you later, Mom."

Mr. Guterman bowed slightly to Grandma Lou. "Madam. It has been a pleasure."

The door closed behind his mother and teacher, and Grandma Lou locked eyes with Wardy. "Your Mr. Guterman—I can see how a person could fall prey to his charm. So vital, so positive, so intense. Yes. I can certainly understand your keen desire to please such a teacher, to follow his every suggestion—even to the exclusion of things you hold important."

"Then—then you think I did the right thing, writing that note to Meg? Now that you've met him, do you think I did the right thing?"

His grandmother wrinkled her brow. "I'd say Mr. Guterman has a very clear perception about his role in your life, your future. Very definite plans. Exciting, wonderful plans. The physics lab, your laser, the Summer Institute . . ."

"Then it *is* right—what Mr. Guterman wants?"

His grandmother appeared to choose her words carefully. "Only you can decide that. Only you. Not Mr. Guterman, not Meg, not me. But I will offer you one thought—and only one."

Wardy watched her face intently. She would tell him what he needed to know to help him think through this dilemma. She had to. He was too mixed-up to think for himself. And this was important. He could feel it in every fiber of his body. It was like coming to a fork in the road and whichever direction you chose would affect you for a long, long time. Because once you chose, there was no going back.

"Mr. Guterman's plans for you, Wardy—his hopes, aspirations. Might they be called ambitions? Ambitions can be lofty, noble, and uplifting, but they can also be destructive. Misdirected. Hurtful. Ambitious people— what motivates them? Think about it. That's all I can suggest to you now. Think about it."

Chapter Fifteen

As irrevocably as Barry had gone out of Wardy's life, he came back in. Without warning, he appeared on the doorstep one Saturday morning, grinning his familiar smile Wardy remembered so well.

"Wh-where did you come from?" Wardy stammered, staring at his old friend.

"You better believe I didn't hitchhike from Fayetteville!" Barry laughed. He pronounced it FAT-*v'll*, Wardy noticed. Barry had picked up a Southern accent. But, otherwise, he seemed exactly the same. Bigger, of course, and older, but his manner was just like it used to be—easy as a summer breeze. The accent fit him perfectly, Wardy decided. It enhanced his relaxed, carefree manner.

"My dad was transferred back here—another two-year hitch, I reckon."

"So, you'll be going to Evanstown High?"

"Uh-huh. Starting Monday. Don't s'pose I'll be in any of your smartass classes, though. Schools down South are behind y'all."

"Hey—why don't you come on in? We can go down to my basement, play around with the laser."

"Nope—can't. Promised Mom I'd help her unpack. We're rentin' two blocks over." He jerked his thumb. "Maybe see y' later this weekend."

"Cool. It'll be like old times, Barry. Two blocks, eh?

You'll be at our bus stop, then."

"Guess so." Barry grinned. One front tooth overlapped the other. It gave him an impish smile. "See y' later, Wardy."

Barry's back. Will we fall into our familiar routines and patterns? So much has happened. He seems the same, but I've changed. I'll never be the old Wardy Spinks again, I hope. Never, never, never.

He closed the door, still thinking. His grandmother motioned him into the kitchen, where she was cleaning up after breakfast.

"Grandma Lou, guess who's back in town to stay? You'll never guess."

"Well, who? I can't imagine."

"Barry. Barry O'Brien—remember him? My best friend—from grade school. We both decided to be research scientists when we grow up."

"That's nice. I liked him, and he was good for you, I remember."

"I still can't believe he's back. It's been over two years, but he seems exactly like before."

"Oh, I doubt that's true," his grandmother said. "You can't go home again, you know. Don't expect too much, and you won't be disappointed."

"What do you mean?"

"Consider how much you've changed in two years. Don't expect any less of Barry. That's all."

Wardy helped clean off the counter. "You mean he may not be interested in catching crayfish and building tree houses anymore?" He chuckled.

"He may not be interested in science anymore—not the way you are. It's become such a focal point for your life—the laser, the science fair, the Summer Youth

Institute—and Mr. Guterman, of course."

Wardy shrugged. "It won't matter. We can still be friends." Reaching for the broom, he began to sweep up toast crumbs.

Grandma Lou surveyed the room. "There. Everything seems shipshape. Now I've got to get packing."

"Already?" Wardy jerked around in surprise. "You're leaving already? You just got here."

"That's true. But Vanessa Franklin—you know, my agent—called this morning. She says it's time to get ready for my next show. It's going to take a lot of preparation. New York. Uptown. It's the gig I've always dreamed about—a one-man show in a very important gallery. I leave from the beach house in a week."

Wardy hugged his grandmother. "That's terrific. New York! Wow! You've really made it to the top, haven't you? Why didn't you tell us sooner?"

"Call it superstition. I've known about this for months, but I'm always afraid to talk about something good until it's a reality. You know what makes me even happier? Seeing *you* enjoying life as you should—with friends and interests and activities. It's the best part for me right now." She patted his shoulder. "I only wish there was room in your life for both Mr. Guterman *and* your friend Meg Reilly. I have a feeling you're missing something good. Now, I must get busy." She hurried out of the kitchen.

Why? Why do the two most important people in my life have to be at odds? Meg doesn't trust Guterman, and Guterman thinks Meg is an unnecessary distraction. Is there any way to have them both?

Barry was right about not being in Wardy's classes.

Monday Wardy saw him in the hall once and in the cafeteria. As usual, Barry was immediately surrounded by people. He was like a magnet in a field of iron filings. But Wardy didn't know any of Barry's new cohorts very well. They were all a part of what Wardy thought of as the "casual crowd." Not too serious about anything; studies, sports, even dating. Everything, it seemed, was done on a whim, without any plan or purpose. *Casual.* That summed it up in a word.

It was not until later that Wardy found out Barry had been placed in Wardy's old Latin class to finish out the year he'd started at his former school. One morning at the bus stop, Barry began talking about Mrs. Burnett being deaf as a post.

"When do you have Latin?" Wardy asked, his curiosity piqued.

"Fifth hour."

"There's a girl in your class I wrote to you about. Meg. Meg Reilly."

"Oh, yeah. I know who she is. She's cute, pal. But awful quiet, don't you think? Are you going with her, or what?"

Going with her. Barry made it sound so—well, casual. That word again. "No. She won't even talk to me now. Someday when you have a couple of hours, I'll tell you why." Meg would never be a part of the casual crowd Barry fit in with so easily. Everything Meg did had deliberation printed all over it. For some reason the thought gave Wardy a good feeling. "Hey, Barry. When y' coming over to see my basement lab? I've got a cool experiment going on."

"Oh...sometime, I guess." He appeared supremely uninterested. "I'm kind of out of the experimental stage now." He laughed, then added, "When it comes to chemistry, anyway. Or is it physics?" He yawned.

"I'm building a laser y' know. I call her Big Vi — short for *Violet*. Mr. Guterman's working on finding me a meter to measure the watt power. I think it's close to 500 watts, from what I can figure."

"Who's Mr. Guterman?"

"Huh?"

"Mr. Guterman. Who's he?" Barry raised his eyebrows.

"You haven't heard about Guterman yet? The exchange teacher?" Wardy was incredulous.

With a bored expression, Barry tossed a rock at the bus stop sign. "Man, I don't care about *teachers*. I'm just interested in chicks. That's all." He yawned again. "Up too late last night, I guess."

Wardy appraised his old friend. Barry's hair was uncombed, and his clothes were rumpled, his eyes rimmed with red.

"You go out last night?"

"Yeah, me and some of my new friends. Went up to the mall and smoked a few."

Wardy started. "Smoked a few? You mean— joints?" His voice rose.

Barry cautioned Wardy in pantomime to quiet down. "Hey, man. Don't tell the world, okay? It's cool. No prob. We're meeting again tonight. Why don't you come along?"

Wardy shook his head. "So, you got into drugs, in the South?"

"It's not drugs. Just a little grass now and then. We scrape up the bread and buy a bag and get mellow. That's all."

Skeptically, Wardy regarded his old friend. He'd never figured Barry to get mixed up with pot. He might appear the same, but he'd changed in more ways than Wardy had bargained for. *And I thought I was the one who'd taken a new road. Ha. Grandma Lou was more right than she'll ever know.*

"Well, if you decide you'd like to share some. . .uh. . .mellow moments, Wardy, give me a call. Okay?"

"Thanks anyway—no interest in getting high." He watched the school bus loom on the horizon.

"Too bad. It's a blast, man. A real blast."

****

Wardy had a hard time concentrating on Mr. Guterman's diagrams. The two had been working on the application of laser technology to missile defense systems, and they were down to the minute details, with a lot of math and complicated formulas. Wardy's mind kept sliding back to Meg. She hadn't given in an inch, but the droop of her shoulders and the downcast expression of her face spelled misery.

"Wardy!" Mr. Guterman spoke sharply. "I can see you are having trouble with this concept. I suggest you take these materials home with you tonight and read them over carefully. We will work on them tomorrow during the tutorial. This is absolutely vital to your attending the Summer Youth Institute."

Standing up, Wardy began an apology. "Sorry. I can't seem to concentrate on math today."

"Math, like science, requires complete concentration. You must train your mind to dwell only on the important matters when they are to be studied and learned. Tune out the inconsequential. It is a form of mental discipline one must acquire to become a first-rate student of science." His eyes held Wardy's; his voice stung with criticism.

Give me time, Guterman— time. I sent Meg away, but I can't sweep her from my thoughts like a pile of dust. Can you understand that? She's still stuck in my mind.

Wardy gathered his books and papers from around him, but Mr. Guterman motioned him to be seated.

"Not yet, Wardy. I have something to tell you. I have received some important information I thought you might be interested in." The teacher fastened his intense gaze on Wardy. "I have recently found out that there is to be a science and technology exposition at Fordwell University here in town. Actually, I have known about the Sci-Tech Exposition for a good while, but, I just discovered that, for the first time, the university is planning to open the demonstrations to high school students who have a teacher sponsor." Pausing, he allowed Wardy to digest the news. "Your laser," he said firmly. "I think it is the time—the opportune time—to bring the laser out into the open, to demonstrate it to the scientific community. Along with the formulas for the fuel—the mirror designs."

For a long moment, Wardy stared back at the teacher, unsure of how to tell him how he felt. That he wasn't ready yet—not ready to unveil his invention for public scrutiny. Not ready to share Big Vi with the world—his secret that had kept him alive when the rest of his life was crumbling down around him. How could he explain it to Guterman—the cold, realistic scientist? How could he make him understand the personal feelings he had for his laser? Big Vi. She was something Wardy had created on his own. Yes, Dr Lowry had given him important information, but Wardy had acquired that help, too, through his own ingenuity and the Quick-Print stationery. Big Vi was *his* invention. But he didn't know how to tell Mr. Guterman about his almost-human attachment to the glass-and-metal instrument hidden safely in the basement lab.

"What's your decision, Wardy?" the teacher pressed. "What do you think?"

"Wh-when is the exposition?" Wardy stalled for time.

"In two weeks. Very short notice, I realize. But, as your sponsor, I will help you get together anything you need to exhibit the laser. We can use tutorial time to do so. Wardy, you must understand the importance of this gathering. There will be professors—scientists— prominent people from all over the United States. They will be viewing the exhibits, taking note of promising students. It will be excellent exposure."

Still, Wardy hesitated. He had an uneasy feeling that once he let the laser out, let it slip through his grasp, it would no longer be his and his alone.

"...it could be the determining factor, you realize," Mr. Guterman had been talking, but Wardy had not heard him. The smooth, persuasive voice—it must have been the way he'd talked old lady Dawson into letting Wardy drop Latin to be Guterman's lab assistant. "It is the one sure step to qualify you for the Summer Youth Institute in Germany—to be recognized at the Fordwell exhibition for your laser experiment. If the laser gets the attention I think it will at Fordwell University, it could be—how do you say it? It could be your *ticket* to the institute. I feel very sure of that."

"Okay," Wardy heard himself saying. "I can have it ready." He bit his lip. *How? How does Guterman do it to me? Get me to say things I don't mean? He's a wizard—pulling rabbits out of hats. Pulling words out of my mouth.*

"Excellent. Excellent." The expression hung in the air between them. "It is time you received credit for your excellent work." Guterman knew how to get to him—knew how to draw him into the game, solidly on his side. Win one for the coach. A coach. That's what Guterman was, really, by his own admission. Only Wardy wasn't sure he wanted to play the game by Guterman's rules—wasn't even sure he wanted to be on the team.

"Think about it. That's all I can suggest to you now. Think about it."

Chapter Sixteen

"Wardy! I have the most wonderful news. I couldn't wait to call and tell you!" It was Grandma Lou. Wardy could hear the childlike excitement bubbling in her voice even over the long-distance wire. "My opening at the gallery—it's this weekend. Saturday night, to be exact. I want you to come be my witness. You can tell your children and grandchildren, 'Yes, good old Lou. She really did have a one-man show in New York. I know because I was there.' "

"You want me to come to New York? But how? How would I get there. Where would I stay?"

"Shhh. Now be quiet a minute and listen. I've got this all worked out, right down to the last detail. I've already bought a plane ticket for you, and I've reserved a single room right here in the hotel where my agent and I are staying. You can fly up after school on Friday, and by Sunday night—when all the glorious fun is over—you'll be back home, ready for school the next day. Oh, Wardy, we'll go to a Broadway play, stroll in Central Park, shop at the biggest stores imaginable—it's too perfect to be turned down! I was going to invite your mother, but when I thought about it, I knew *you* were the one I wanted most. Now! What do you say?"

"I—can't believe it. That you'd go to all that trouble for me. I'd love to come, but . . ." He stopped. How could he say it? How would tell his grandmother that he was already booked for the weekend—that Guterman was expecting him to demonstrate his laser at the Sci-Tech Exposition at Fordwell University? It was supposed to be *his* debut—his breakthrough in the scientific community. How to tell her?

"But what, Wardy?" Grandma Lou's voice had gone flat—all the bubbles evaporated from the soda. "I hope you didn't already have plans. Oh, I should've checked first. I didn't think…I wanted so much . . ."

"I promised Mr. Guterman I'd go to the Sci-Tech Exposition on Friday and Saturday to demonstrate my laser. He's—Mr. Guterman's counting on me." Wardy felt like a jerk. How could he say the words to his grandmother, who was being kind and generous and thinking of him? He felt about two inches tall.

"Promised Mr. Guterman?" Grandma Lou's voice was thick—as though she were trying to smother the chagrin she felt, trying to sound natural—but Wardy could detect the disappointment behind her words. "I'm sorry, Wardy. Truly. I guess I *will* invite your mother then—to use the plane ticket, the hotel room. I shouldn't be doing things like this at my age—getting my heart set to go before my mind's in gear. Let me speak to Gwen, then. Please don't tell her she's my second choice. It'll be our secret."

"I'm sorry. If I had the option, I'd rather come to New York—to your show. I'd rather be with you, believe me. I'd much rather do that than go to the exposition with Guterman. It's just that . . ."

"I know. I do believe you. Really. Now let me speak to your mom." She sounded like her usual jovial self now. He'd rather she'd sounded dismayed. He was feeling so guilty. "She's not here now. Shall I have her call you when she gets home? She's working late, I think."

"No. I'll call back later tonight. Bye, dear. And don't worry—I'll get over my disappointment. I should have realized you'd be busy with your new, full life."

Guterman. He's doing it again. Putting himself between me and somebody I care about. Forcing me to make a choice. Will it ever end, this conflict with Guterman?

Jamming his hands in his pockets, Wardy kicked open the door and, without thinking, began walking aimlessly down the street. Was it right, could it be right when it felt so completely wrong? Guterman made the exposition sound important, but—the letter to Meg, turning his grandmother down on the most significant event of her life. Did it always have to be Guterman's way? So absorbed was Wardy in his thoughts that in the dim, late-winter twilight, he almost missed Barry, who had crossed the side street ahead of him. Wardy shouted to be heard. "Hey, Barry! Wait up. Barry!"

"Wardy, my friend. What brings you out this time of the evening? Aren't you supposed to have your face in a book or your hands wrapped around a microscope or something?" Barry's overlapping teeth flashed in a comical, crooked grin. He waited for Wardy to catch up, thumbs hooked in his pockets.

"Where are y' going, Barry?" Wardy puffed as he caught his breath and fell in with Barry's stride.

"Meeting some friends at the bowling alley to roll a few . . .uh, frames. Loosen up, y' know? Join us?"

"I haven't got any money with me. Are you guys really going to bowl, or . . .?"

Barry shrugged. "Who knows, man. If it feels good,

do it."

Studying Barry's profile, Wardy blurted, "Barry, how'd you come to—to change so much? I mean, you were always happy-go-lucky, but . . ." He struggled to find the right words. "But you seemed to be involved in things—things that mattered to you. But now . . .now there's no purpose. No direction . . ." Wardy's voice trailed off.

"Yeah, well, you could stand a bit of unraveling yourself, y' know? Shake it out. Life's too short to get hung up on what everybody else wants you to do. Do something for yourself. My advice."

For a few blocks, they walked in silence. Wardy's thoughts churned and thrashed. *What everybody else wants. Everybody else? Or just one person?* Something Grandma Lou had told him a long time ago, on the beach house porch, struggled to surface. With a start, he remembered. *The Pretenders. Don't let the Pretenders take over—ruin your happiness. Guterman? A Pretender? Was it possible?*

"You're awful quiet, Bro. Decide to come along?" They had reached a crossroad at the main intersection in town. "I can lend you the bread, if that's what's bothering you."

"What? No. I'm not coming with you." Wardy turned to retrace his steps back home. With a wave to his old friend, he called out, "Thanks, Barry."

Barry appeared puzzled. "Thanks? Thanks for what?"

"For reminding me of something. Something I needed to remember."

Shrugging, grinning amiably, Barry sauntered off toward the bowling alley and his friends. Wardy set off in a jog in the opposite direction. He had to hurry—had to get home before Grandma Lou called back to make the weekend offer to his mother.

He knew now what he was going to do, and the thought sent simultaneous sparks of delight and fear shooting through him. He sped up like he'd been hot-wired. He was going to New York. Going to renege on his pledge to Mr. Guterman. Grandma Lou was more important. She had to come first. *What'll I tell Guterman? How'll I say it? What'll he do?* His thoughts kept beat to the rhythm of his pumping legs. *Good old wishy-washy, blow-with-the-breeze Barry. He's given me the answer. In his own words, told me what to do. "Life's too short to get hung up on what everybody else wants you to do. Do something for yourself." Shakespeare and Grandma Lou had put it better: "To thine own self be true."*

****

Clamping his teeth on the biggest corned beef sandwich he'd ever seen in his life, Wardy let the sights, sounds, smells of the delicatessen seep into his pores. It was a banquet to be savored and enjoyed. All around him the restaurant clattered and bustled. Voices rose above the scraping of the straight-legged wooden chairs, vying with the clatter of China, thick and white, rattling on huge trays carried by hustling waiters. Above, ceiling fans paddled the tantalizing smells of spice and herbs around the dining room. From his seat, he could peer out the smoky plate glass window and see the city action framed for a moment. It was like seeing through the lens of a camera in which the picture kept changing.

Wardy grinned at his grandmother. "This is terrific. You were right. There's nothing like a New York deli for real atmosphere. Real food."

"Louise, does this boy always eat like a stevedore?" It was Vanessa Franklin, his grandmother's agent. They were having a quick bite before Wardy's plane was to take him back to Evanstown—the real world.

"He's done the local cuisine ample justice this weekend, Van, I'll grant you that." Grandma Lou smiled indulgently. "Let's see. Bagels for breakfast, New York pizza for lunch, and I expect he'd like some bona fide cheesecake for dessert once he's finished that monster of a sandwich."

"Other than food, Wardy—and your grandmother's show—what would you call the highlight of your trip to the Big Apple?" Miss Franklin seemed genuinely interested in his answer.

"Getting lost in the subway," Wardy chuckled. "It's a sure way to learn the difference between uptown and downtown—fast."

"Was the Broadway musical dazzling enough for you?" Miss Franklin was not yet satisfied he'd had a great time.

"Oh, yeah. The costumes, the dancing—they were awesome. And the live orchestra below stage—it was…well, I've never seen anything like it." Wardy turned to his grandmother. "I guess I've got a lot to thank you for. You went to so much trouble for me this weekend."

"My pleasure, Wardy. You were my witness."

"Your exhibit. My own grandmother—the star of the show. I'll be witness to that anytime."

"I was shocked at how many people attended," Grandma Lou said.

Wardy nodded. "They adored your work. I listened

to them talk in the gallery—so many artists. They sure think you're someone special. Every one of them."

"Your grandmother would never tell you this herself, but she's helped many of those people somewhere along the way at one time or another in their lives." Miss Franklin's tone was low and confiding. "An important introduction here, a helpful little note of encouragement there—and more than a few 'anonymous' cash gifts to tide over a starving artist. Lou believes in sharing the wealth—the wealth of knowledge and understanding she's developed in the world of fine arts. Artists can be a solitary lot, Wardy, but we never forget a favor from a colleague."

His grandmother chuckled. "Vanessa tends to hyperbole. Remember, I've been around art circles for a long, long time. You meet a lot of people over the years, form close relationships." She nodded. "Wardy! You're fidgeting like a cat in a cage. Whatever is going through that amazing mind of yours now?"

"I was just wondering how Mr. Guterman feels about that. Mr. Guterman says people come in last. Science is first. He's wrong, isn't he?"

"Mr. Guterman is a very determined man. A man with clear goals. If they've narrowed him—made him one-dimensional—that's his loss. But it doesn't have to affect you. He has no share in your ego. Satisfying his requirements won't naturally lead to your own gratification."

"You should have seen him when I told him I wouldn't be showing my laser at the Sci-Tech Exposition."

"Angry?"

"Furious would be more like it. Cold, enraged. He

could only talk about all the influential people I'd miss if I skipped out." Wardy gulped. "But if people aren't important, how come Guterman was so furious I'd miss the influential ones?"

"Ambition overload can warp one's values sometimes. I suspect Mr. Guterman might have been more interested in the influential people for his own purposes and edification, rather than yours."

"You mean he thinks he can benefit from my work on the laser? Since he's my 'mentor' as Mom calls him?" The idea struck Wardy as highly irregular.

"That's exactly what I think." Grandma Lou nodded.

"But, Guterman—he had nothing to do with the laser. It was already completed when he saw it for the first time in my lab. How could he hope to take any credit?"

"You've just hit the nail on the head. He's the mentor, you're the protégé. Don't you see? Nothing need ever be said—the implication alone would be enough. You were to demonstrate the laser, and he was your teacher-sponsor, right?"

"It's hard to believe he—he'd use me like that." Wardy's voice rang hollow with doubt. "Do you really think . . .?"

"I think it's quite likely."

"Lou, Wardy," Miss Franklin said. "You'll have to excuse me now. I have an appointment at five, so I'm going to catch a taxi and dash. See you again soon, I hope, Wardy. So glad you came. I know Lou is, too."

Wardy stood up. "Bye, Miss Franklin. Thanks for all your tour-guiding." They watched her hurry out the door and into the street, caught for a moment in the frame of the window before she was gone.

Across the table, they observed each other. "Well, it's almost over, my—our—big weekend. It's made me realize a few things I've been skirting for some time." Her face had softened to match her voice. Wardy blinked rapidly. His alarm bells went off. Something was amiss.

"I've felt myself slowing down this past year. Not voluntarily—it's just something your body does to you. And . . .and last week my doctor confirmed my suspicions. 'Lou, it's time you took a vacation—thought about retirement. Why don't you give that beach house of yours a permanent occupant. *You*.' "

"But, New York! Just when you've made it to the top—to quit?"

"Not quit. Just slow down. I'll still go on with my life, but I won't take on so much. Because I *have* achieved a lifelong ambition. It's okay to give myself a little rest."

His grandmother's smooth pink cheeks, her pleasant smile made it hard to think of her as old. She had so much vitality, so much sparkle and fun in her. But her eyes. For the first time, he noticed how tired they were. He had to admit it to himself, his grandmother was not immortal. Her hectic travel schedule couldn't go on forever. "You know best. And it will be nice to visit you at the beach house whenever I want—knowing you'll be there."

"Yes. Won't that be fun?" Her weary eyes brightened. "But, I want you to remember always: There are people all around you, people you can go to. Your friends. Your own mother and father. Mr. Guterman is wrong, you know. It's the people in life that give it meaning and value."

People. Yes. Mom and Dad? Mr. Guterman? My

friends? What about Meg Reilly? She's the one I really want to go to. But I can't. There's this gap between us— a gap caused by my own stupidity. Meg. You're the one I need.

Chapter Seventeen

All hope of sleep gone, Wardy lay on his bed, hands clasped behind his neck. Scenes played over and over in his mind. Guterman's first day in biology class. His job as lab assistant to Guterman. Tutorials. Guterman when he saw Big Vi. The Summer Youth Institute. He couldn't turn them off, and he couldn't get around the fact that his life had become much sweeter since Mr. Guterman had entered it. For once he felt like a regular guy. Nobody had played a practical joke on him lately. The cyber-bullying hardly bothered him anymore. All the old graffiti—Wardy Spinks Is Eaglebait—fading from the walls and lockers. Because he was *somebody* now. He was Mr. Guterman's lab assistant. Mr. Guterman's protégé. Mr. Gutterman's top GT student.

A mentor, his mother had called Guterman. He'd found the word in his dictionary: "a wise and trusted teacher, guide, and friend." It was the perfect description of Heinrich Guterman—only Wardy wasn't sure he was "trusted" anymore. And something else had happened. Wardy wasn't just grateful anymore for Mr. Guterman's guidance. No—it had gone beyond that. Now it was more like indebted. Obligated. Wardy had begun to feel he had to justify Mr. Guterman's interest in him. How had it happened, the subtle change? And when?

Doubt clouded his mind. What should he do about the teacher? Guterman was bound to call him into his office tomorrow after biology class. It would, no doubt, be Wardy's last chance to make it up to Guterman—for leaving him in the lurch with the Sci-Tech Exposition. Should Wardy go crawling back, like some low-life worm from the bio lab? Promise to return and be a good, obedient little boy again—promise to do Guterman's bidding in order to get the all-important pat on the head he'd come to rely on? Would Guterman even *have* him back? Or, once that frozen façade thawed away, would something even colder, tougher, more resistant be revealed? What might be exposed once the rigidly controlled exterior melted away? Wardy shivered at the possibilities.

Why couldn't he cheerfully accept everything that was happening? Any other kid would be proud—jump at the chance to demonstrate an experiment in front of a lot of high-level professionals. His grades were up in all his subjects—he was going to Europe for the summer. How many fourteen-year-old boys got that kind of opportunity? The prestige of the Summer Youth Institute was incredible. Wardy had done a thorough Internet search and read all about it. His trip would be announced to the whole school in the spring awards assembly Guterman said. So, why not go slinking back, beg forgiveness, plead insanity—get back in Guterman's good graces?

Swinging his legs over the side of the bed, Wardy sat up. It was two in the morning. The sheets were a wreck—all wrapped and twisted as if they'd just come out of the washing machine. Tiptoeing to the closet, he hastily donned his bathrobe, then stealthily made his way down the stairs to the basement lab. Carefully, he closed and bolted the door before turning on the overhead fluorescent light. In the blue-white gleam, the clear glass tube of the laser glittered transparently. For a while, he tinkered with the mirrors that lay unassembled on the workbench. How he had worked over these mirror designs, painstakingly arranging them to resemble Dr. Lowry's diagrams. How excited he had been when he was able to direct the powerful beam the way he wanted it to go, harnessing all that potency. Directing, manipulating, guiding something so forceful and destructive—that was part of the excitement of his laser experiment. It was also part of the reason he was reluctant to let it go, to allow someone else—Guterman—to bask in the glow of his accomplishment.

For a long time, he puttered around Big Vi. It soothed him to be able to fix his mind on something concrete and tangible—to wipe out the tumultuous speculations flashing on and off in his thoughts like an arcade sign. *This is crazy. I ought to get back to bed—get some sleep. I'll worry about Guterman tomorrow.* Turning off the lab light, locking the door, he made his way back to his room, where he crawled under the tangled sheets. *Sleep. Sleep. Sleep.* Turning on his side, he fell into a light doze. Suddenly, he flinched violently. He'd been dreaming of something—something that had been trying to rise to the surface of his consciousness all night. It was the thought of Meg. Yes, Meg—that was when Guterman began to change. *When I dismissed Meg according to Guterman's wishes—like a robot programmed to do the master's bidding. That's when it happened. That's when Guterman took over. She saw it coming—sensitive, shy, quiet, intelligent Meg. She knew all along—tried to tell me—but I tossed her out. Fell into the trap. Why didn't I listen to her?*

No wonder Meg had taken it so hard—the way Guterman had deliberately separated them in every way possible. And then his own note of dismissal. Guterman's domination. She could see it all so clearly, and she'd tried to help him see. With Meg in the way, Guterman couldn't be sure of complete control over him. But Wardy had gone blindly along with the teacher. Now he knew what he would do tomorrow. There was no longer any question about it. He rolled over and fell instantly asleep.

The day crawled by. Every minute lasted two hours, Wardy decided, glancing at the big, flat school wall clock for the hundredth time. Fifth period wouldn't be over for fifteen more minutes. Fifteen minutes until biology class, where he would see Meg. Talk to her, if he could. Try to explain. Before class, during, after—it didn't matter. He had to start somewhere—had to break through the barrier of silence she'd built. With Guterman watching over the whole drama, it would make even more of a point in his favor, he hoped. At last, the bell released him from the stuffy physics lab where he'd been working on an experiment at the back table. Mr. Guterman acted as if everything was the same, but Wardy knew there would be words before the day was over. Behind the German's strong, square jaw, he could sense a chilling tension, a cold determination.

Luck was with him. He spied Meg in the hall outside the biology room, and she was alone. Her soft brown hair had fallen into her eyes as she rummaged through her purse for something. She did not see him approach.

"Meg? Meg, can we talk?" It was the only beginning he could think of, despite his many rehearsed openings. His voice sounded thin, even to his own ears.

Jerking her head up, Meg fixed him with her dark eyes. "Talk about what, Wardy? I don't think there's anything to talk about." Her whispery voice fell in gentle waves on his ears.

"But there is, Meg. There is. I have so much to tell you—so much I want to tell you. That is, if you'll listen. I've been wrong, you know. Terribly wrong."

She lowered her eyes, so that all he could see was the dark fringe of her lashes resting on her cheeks. "It's all over between us. The friendship—it can never be the same again." Her voice was even quieter than usual— barely audible—but it sent hot needles through him, stabbing pains of reality. She was so sensitive. Too sensitive. Couldn't she forgive—forget? The tardy bell rang.

"I have to get to class now," Meg whispered. "I don't like to be late for Guterman's class." Noiselessly, she stepped in front of him and slid through the door while he stood with his mouth gaping, unnerved and speechless. It was going to be difficult to win her back. She'd been hurt, and she wasn't going to get over it quickly. But he had to try again—to keep trying. She meant too much to give up now.

In class, Mr. Guterman was at his brilliant best. He was all over the room with his eyes, his voice, probing with his electrifying questions. Lightning flashed in the supercharged atmosphere of the biology room as ideas caught fire and flared like bright torches in the dusty, stuffy air. *He's a genius. He really is. A genius of a teacher. He knows how to grab us, hold us, keep us. Use our minds. Use us.* The bell rang, and Wardy's heart leapt into his throat.

"Wardy?" Mr. Guterman never raised his voice in

class. He didn't have to. His classes always ended in hushed, reverent quiet. "I would like to see you in my office today after school, please." Nodding, Wardy gathered up his books, sliding a glance toward Meg's lab table across the room. But she kept her back to him, no doubt deliberately. Okay. He'd lost round one. But he wasn't finished yet. This was one fight he was willing to battle to the bitter end.

Scooting his chair under the table, Wardy lifted his books and pushed through the room. For the first time that hour, he was aware of the hissing of the radiator at his back. Hissing like Guterman's *s's*. *Hissing a warning: H-s-s-s-s! Watch out, Wardy Spinks. Your time has come.* It weakened his resolve, distracted him from the purpose. *H-s-s-s-s. It's not going to be so easy, Spinks-s-s-s.* The time had come at last; his determination ebbed, subsiding with every step in the direction of Guterman's office.

The teacher sat at his desk, reading. Wardy took his customary seat, but Guterman did not stir. After several tense minutes, he raised his eyes, directing his bold, steady gaze at Wardy, breaking the silence. "I attended the Sci-Tech Exposition at Fordwell University over the weekend. You are interested in hearing about it, yes?" His blue eyes glinted icily.

Dumbly, Wardy nodded, not trusting his voice.

"It was very enlightening. Very." Mr. Guterman's clipped voice was frigid. "An experience you should not have missed."

If he gave just one little smile—just one—he'd crack into tiny, brittle pieces. Something has to warm the man up, or he'll freeze into a solid lump of blue ice right behind his desk. Starting with his eyes and working outward.

"I-I'd like to hear about it. If you'd care to tell me."
So far so good. Haven't tried to apologize yet. Resist the urge. Keep strong. Keep cool. Out-freeze him.

Guterman continued, his voice growing more agitated with each word. "It was an amazing aggregation of avant-garde technology and scientific invention. But there was nothing, *nothing* that even approached your laser in technological sophistication. Certainly not in the high school division—not on the college level, either." He was warming up, all right, hissing like the radiator in the biology room. The cold exterior had steamed off, allowing Wardy to see the angry interior for the first time. The intensity was alarming—alarming in its violence. "If you had been there—if you had demonstrated your fuel, the power of your laser, the sophistication of its directional ability—you would have taken all the honors. Earned a name for yourself. Assured yourself a place at the Summer Youth Institute. Make no mistake: It was an opportunity lost for you."

Wardy noticed that Mr. Guterman was shaking. His hands trembled and his cheeks flushed redder with every breath. He shook with fury. He was not through. His voice rose in a long, slow crescendo.

"For what did you miss this—this important exposition? For what? To go see an old grandmother who couldn't wait for another time—for *any* other time to have you present? Was it a fair exchange? Are you proud of the decision you made—made in defiance of me?" His voice strained—as close to a shout as Wardy had ever heard the teacher get. He'd thawed out. Smoldering rage had melted all the ice.

"When I think of the influential people who came to

Fordwell and what they could have seen, with what ideas they would have left the exposition, I—I...To think that all my work here—that I've wasted so much on one person. On *you*, Wardy Spinks. And you turned on me— failed me—when it all would have counted most." Violently now, his hands trembled. Wardy feared his fury would erupt uncontrollably, like a volcano. For a long time, the teacher appeared to war within himself, trying to calm his rage. When he spoke again, it was almost with a sense of exhaustion. But the anger still flared in his bright eyes. "Do you have any idea how wide a sphere of influence is wielded by the scientists and professionals gathered at Fordwell this weekend? Do you know how highly they are regarded in academic circles? In industry?"

With clear insight, Wardy realized how important these influential people might be to Guterman's own career. Was this why he had been pressing so hard for Wardy to participate in the exhibition? Had Grandma Lou been right?

Guterman wasn't finished. "Do you realize the prestige there could be in the future—to be affiliated with such renowned individuals? William Norton of MIT. Yes. He was there. Professor Andrew Stanislov of Stanford. Dr. Robert Lowry . . ."

Wardy started. Dr. Robert Lowry? *His* Dr. Lowry? Was it possible? Suddenly finding his voice, he broke in on Guterman's bitter raving. "Did you say Dr. Robert Lowry? The research scientist from Cal/Tech? You mean Dr. Lowry was at the Sci-Tech Exposition?"

"How would you know anything about such a distinguished personage?" Guterman snarled. His face had mottled to a slow burn, his voice the harsh rasp of a metal file.

Abruptly, Wardy stood up. "Mr. Guterman, I have to leave now. I didn't want to disappoint you about the Sci-Tech Exposition—I really didn't. But my grandmother needed me. She's more important to me than anything else in the world. *Anything.*"

It wasn't exactly what he'd planned to say, after all, but it would have to suffice. He had something else to do—to do fast, before Dr. Lowry had a chance to leave Evanstown, if he hadn't already headed back to the West Coast. Wardy had to get in touch with him. If only he'd known sooner that Dr. Lowry was in town. Wardy headed toward the door.

"Where are you going?" Guterman asked. His cold voice had returned.

"I have some research to do—some very important research. Good-bye, Mr. Guterman." Realizing he'd left his phone at home, he opened the office door and left. In the corridor, he took off running. *Jog fast, jog fast, jog fast.* He drilled himself as he sprinted out the school doors and down the street. *Got to get home, find a phone number for Fordwell, find out where Dr. Lowry's staying. Hope I'm not too late. Not too late. Not too late. Jog fast, jog fast, jog fast.* He concentrated on the rhythm. The rhythm would get him home.

Panting, exhausted, he slammed through his front door and tossed his backpack onto the floor, trying to catch his breath enough to climb the stairs to his room to get his phone. Focused as he was on his mission, he'd missed the rental car parked in the driveway—missed the fact that his mother was already home, sitting in the living room talking to someone. Gradually, as the buzzing in his ears subsided and his heartbeats calmed, he realized that something was up. Something unusual.

"Mom?" Hesitantly, he rounded the corner into the living room. "Mom?"

His mother sat on the sofa, a tea service on the table in front of her. Comfortably seated in the armchair was a pleasant-faced middle-aged man with silver-gray hair and a short beard. He wore wire-rimmed glasses and held a pipe to his lips.

"Wardy, come in. Catch your breath. I have a surprise for you," his mother said.

Curiously, almost afraid to breathe, Wardy made his way into the room. He glanced tentatively at the gentleman in the armchair.

"Wardy, I'd like you to meet Dr. Robert Lowry. From California. He called me at the office today, and I invited him over for tea. It seems you two know each other—sort of."

"D-Dr. Lowry? Oh. You're sitting in my living room! Dr. Lowry from Cal/Tech—in my own living room!" Wardy's eyebrows shot straight up.

Dr. Lowry threw back his silvery head and laughed heartily. "I'm not a ghost. It's really me. Sit down. We have a lot to talk about."

Chapter Eighteen

"The mirrors, ha, ha! They are perfect! You've coated them with linseed oil, you say?" Dr. Lowry had spent the past hour scrutinizing Wardy's laser in minute detail. "And 500 watts of power. Hmmm...may I see your calculations?"

Wardy scrambled to find his worksheets.

For a while, Dr. Lowry examined the papers. "Yes," he said at length. "This seems accurate. I don't suppose you'd be willing to cook up some of the fuel—the hexafluoride—and show me how it works?"

"You're planning to stay a while, then? If you do, we could fuel the laser later tonight." Wardy trembled with excitement. "Nobody's ever seen what Big Vi can do except me." He laughed self-consciously. "Big Vi's her nickname. Short for Violet. I almost think of her as—as a friend. I've spent so many hours working down here with her."

Dr. Lowry smiled approvingly. "Quite right. I know the feeling myself. I sometimes get so attached to my own work that my wife thinks she's got a rival—a rival in the lab."

There was a light tap on the lab door. Wardy opened it a crack and peeked out. It was his mother. "Wardy, I wondered if Dr. Lowry would like to stay for dinner. It's getting rather late, and he's most welcome to stay." On impulse, because he was feeling expansive, Wardy opened the door wide. "Why don't you come in and talk to him yourself?"

Stepping into the lab for the first time, Gwen gazed around, wide-eyed at what she saw. "Why—I had no idea you were working with such—such sophisticated equipment in here." Her eyes rested on the laser. "What is it? It seems quite official."

"It's a laser, Mom. Big Vi. I've been working on her for months." He hung his head. "You don't know it, but I heat the ingredients for the fuel in the microwave."

Startled, Gwen put a hand to her chest. "Heavens! Is that safe?" She turned to Dr. Lowry, who watched the scene with an amused expression.

"I'd say if Wardy's in charge, you should have no fears. He's a fine scientist. Very thorough."

His mother appeared at a loss for words. "I honestly had no idea such high-level experimentation was going on under my own roof," she managed at last. "I just thought Wardy was doing cutesy little things down here. You know, laughing gas or something. I know Heinrich Guterman, his science teacher, was impressed, but I had no idea, really. I'm flabbergasted."

Judging from his broad smile and occasional chuckles, Dr. Lowry appeared to enjoy the whole scene immensely. "Wardy's brought off this experiment very much on his own merits. I feel honored to have been able to offer useful input. But Big Vi is Wardy's and Wardy's alone. You can be proud of your son, Mrs. Spinks. Very proud."

"Well. Thank you, Dr. Lowry. I'm beginning to see that. It's a new side of my son—a side I never imagined was there."

"Are you going to invite Dr. Lowry to dinner, Mom?

Isn't that what you came down here for?"

"Oh, yes. Please do stay, Dr. Lowry. I'm sure you and Wardy have much to talk about, and I—well, I shall simply listen."

"Can we borrow the microwave one more time? Dr. Lowry wants to watch me make the fuel."

"Of course. Anything in the name of science." She turned to the door, looking as though someone had just thrown a surprise party for her. "Dinner in a half hour," she said as she left.

Wardy showed Dr. Lowry the holes in the workroom wall that he had patched. "I'll tell my mom about these later. Not sure she's ready for another surprise yet."

Dr. Lowry nodded. "Probably a good idea."

Dinner was a fascinating experience. Dr. Lowry was a lively conversationalist who kept the topics current and interesting. Even Leslie, whose class had been studying energy conservation, got involved in a discussion of nuclear power plants. Wardy couldn't remember tasting a single thing on his plate, though everyone else complimented his mother on the delicious dinner. Dr. Lowry was not only a brilliant scientist, Wardy realized, but also a down-to-earth guy, interested in pro football and television programs and all sorts of other things normal people liked to talk about.

"So, Mrs. Spinks, when Wardy wrote to me about his laser—well, I couldn't wait to write back to see what he'd accomplished. Most people don't realize that important scientific breakthroughs can occur far outside the sterile, controlled atmosphere of the professional laboratory."

"Dr. Lowry." A question nudged at the edges of

Wardy's thoughts, and at last he'd gathered the nerve to ask it. "Will you tell me the truth if I ask you a kind of personal question?"

Pausing with his fork midway in the air over his plate, Dr. Lowry seemed intrigued. "Artifice is not one of my talents, Wardy. Fire away. I'll tell it like it is." His eyes crinkled in merriment.

"The first time I wrote to you and you wrote back accepting me as Dr. Spinks, professor of nuclear physics, did you know—did you suspect then that I was just a kid? I mean, I practiced writing so that it would sound like a professional business letter—come across like a real scientist's—but did you know then or not?"

The professor's eyes danced, and he chuckled. "I wondered if you'd ever get around to that question. I knew from the beginning that my writer was not an adult. I knew he couldn't possibly be old enough to be a professor of anything. But a 'real scientist,' as you put it—absolutely. I knew I was dealing with a real scientist, and that's why I answered you." Dr. Lowry paused to take a breath. "There's one more thing, Wardy. When you finally wrote to tell me the truth about yourself— that told me something very important about your character. Something I was glad to know."

Gwen followed the professor's words with the same stunned expression Wardy had noticed in his lab. It was as though she was seeing him—really seeing him—for the first time.

Basking in the glow of Dr. Lowry's complimentary words, Wardy almost missed the professor's next statement. "Now, I know how you feel about Big Vi. But I want you to consider very seriously a proposal I am going to make. I will respect your decision, of course."

All eyes at the table were on Dr. Lowry. "After I've watched you formulate the fuel, if I think there's any future in it—and I feel very positive about that now or I wouldn't bring it up—what I'd like is for you to write an article for a scientific journal put out by our university press. An article, complete with diagrams, about your laser, your fuel, every detail, the works. Put some of that writing ability of yours to better use. What do you think?"

"It would be a great challenge for me, Dr. Lowry. I'd really like to try."

"Wonderful, wonderful! Actually, there's a little plum attached to the assignment, but I purposely didn't mention it—didn't want to sound as though I were trying to entice you into writing the article."

"A plum?"

"The university has a summer workshop for scientifically gifted youth. Each year we award scholarships—all expenses paid—for the best articles submitted. The journal is called *Science Now*. It is completely student-written."

"The workshop—what's it like?"

"It's held right on the university campus. You'd have access to all the facilities—pools, gyms, courts. You'd stay in a dormitory and attend classes taught by our professors. That's in the mornings. Afternoons are reserved for field trips, labs in the research facility, guest speakers. At night there's a lot of hobnobbing among the workshop students—parties, games, dances. Plenty of activities for everyone."

"It sounds too good to be true," his mother said. "But I'm afraid Wardy's already involved in plans to attend the Summer Youth . . ." She stopped when she heard the doorbell. "My goodness. Who could that . . .oh no! I forgot! In all the excitement of Dr. Lowry's visit, I completely forgot my date with Heinrich." Hurriedly, she left the table, returning moments later with Mr. Guterman. "Heinrich. Heinrich Guterman," she said a little unsteadily. "I'd like you to meet Dr. Robert Lowry. He's here to see Wardy—and his laser."

Wardy watched Mr. Guterman's face turn to stone. Gray, flat, hard, and cold. He offered a handshake in greeting, but his expression remained rocklike. "A pleasure, sir. Have you known Wardy for a long time, then?"

"Only on paper," Dr. Lowry said enigmatically, ignoring Mr. Guterman's granite demeanor. "Wardy and I have been corresponding for some time about his experiments. When I found I was to be in his hometown for the Sci-Tech Exposition, naturally I wanted to meet him."

"I see," Mr. Guterman said. "In that case, I'll not interrupt you." He turned to Gwen and bowed slightly. "Another time, perhaps?" For just a moment his eyes locked onto Wardy with an expression that Wardy had never before seen. Regret? Dismay? Wardy couldn't put his finger on it, and it was gone in an instant. "Good-bye, Dr. Lowry," Mr. Guterman said. He turned on his heel and was gone.

"Well," Gwen breathed, reseating herself. "Heinrich seemed a bit moody tonight. He'll get over it. Europeans can be quite punctilious, I've discovered. I don't think he liked my forgetting our date."

"Can we get back to the *Science Now* article?" Wardy asked abruptly.

"We have an excellent graphic artist who will be

glad to prepare any diagrams you'd want to include. As I said, the writings are all done by students who have the opportunity to work with the illustrator."

Wardy's mind had been moving rapidly, jumping from thought to thought like a racer in a maze. "Dr. Lowry, I think I can get a friend of mine to do the diagrams—and I bet they'll be as good as your artist's."

"Is this friend a student, Wardy? That would be even better for our journal's purpose."

"She's my age—and she used to be my lab partner in biology. If it hadn't been for her diagrams…Well, our reports wouldn't have been half as successful." *Better late than never, Meg. Your work is finally getting some due praise.*

"Splendid, Wardy. I think that covers everything. Now, let's help your mother with these dishes and get on with our own cooking. What do you say?"

Wardy gave the professor a bright smile. "Dessert, Dr. Lowry?"

Two hours later, Wardy and Dr. Lowry stood in the chilly backyard surveying their handiwork. They had moved Big Vi, piece by piece, out of the basement workroom. A beaker of hexafluoride compound sat cooling on the picnic table beside the laser where they'd reassembled the parts. Wardy had turned the backyard floodlight onto their work area so that they could easily see under the bright cone of light. They both shook with cold and excitement. Dr. Lowry was just like a kid, Wardy decided. He seemed as enthusiastic as Wardy about watching Big Vi do her thing. He kept rubbing his hands together and saying things like, "Get ready for the big boom. Here it comes."

Dr. Lowry drew an object from the pocket of his

coat, holding it aloft so Wardy could discern its identity in the beaming arc of the floodlight. It was a can of beans. Pork and beans. Wardy was mystified.

"I hope your mother won't mind," he said with an impish grin. "I borrowed it from her pantry when you were working with the formula. I thought we'd better give Vi a good target. What do you think, Wardy? Can she make it all the way to that fence post over there?" He pointed beyond the picnic table to the edge of the yard.

"Easily," Wardy said with assurance. He took the can from Dr. Lowry and placed it carefully on the post, then went to the picnic table and positioned the laser for a direct hit. "Would you like to activate the fuel, Dr. Lowry?" Wardy knew full well the professor would like nothing better.

"Could I?" His eyes lit up, and he stroked his beard excitedly.

"You're as gung-ho about this experiment as I am," Wardy couldn't help saying to the professor.

"You bet! Nothing more exciting than the frontiers of scientific discovery." He rubbed his hands together again as if trying to warm them. "Okay, Wardy. Here goes." He pulled the trigger of the strobe light, and they watched intently as a thin beam of violet light plowed through the night air. A red spot the size of a quarter appeared on the label around the can of beans, and instantly they smelled the acrid burning of paper. No! It was the smell of burning beans, Wardy realized. Eyes widening, he stared as steam poured out of a hole in the can. Then, as if some strange, wild, trapped being was trying to push its way out of the can, every seam in the metal burst open, spewing blackened, crusty beans and pork in a splattering, ear-shattering explosion.

Gwen appeared at the back door, obviously concerned. Leslie stood beside her, her eyes big and luminous in the floodlights. Backyard lights from neighbors around the periphery of the yard flared like fireflies on the horizon. "Wardy? Is everything all right?" his mother asked. "What was the noise? Do I smell smoke?"

Wardy and Dr. Lowry had been doing a little two-step dance around the picnic table, but they stopped long enough for the professor to call out an answer. "Don't worry, Mrs. Spinks. Everything's fine. You just heard the sound of real science in progress. That's all."

"Way to go, Big Vi," Wardy cheered. "Way to go."

Chapter Nineteen

"I still find it hard to believe my microwave had a part in your laser experiment," his mother said. Dr. Lowry had gone, Leslie was in bed, and together the two of them cleaned up the kitchen. She leaned over the dishwasher, removing clean plates and glasses, setting them on the counter. At the sink, Wardy rinsed out the sponge and then returned to the microwave with renewed vigor. "In fact, Wardy, all in all, I think this evening has opened my eyes to any number of things I've been ignoring—for too long." She sat on a tall stool behind the kitchen counter. "Are you finished yet? I'd like to heat myself a cup of tea."

"All done." He filled a mug with water and set it in the oven. "Will a minute do it?"

His mother nodded. "Thanks. Why don't you make yourself a cup of cocoa while you're at it?"

Together they sat at the counter, their steaming mugs in front of them. "Wardy," his mother said reflectively, "how do you feel about Heinrich Guterman? Can you give me an honest opinion?"

"He's a great teacher. I'll probably never be lucky enough to study under anyone like him again. He knows all the right things to do to make a kid learn."

"I'm glad you've had the opportunity. But what of his role as mentor? How do you feel about that?"

"Mom, can I ask *you* a question?"

174

"Of course."

"How do *you* feel about Mr. Guterman? I mean, do you see him taking Dad's place sometime, maybe?"

His mother's tone reflected her interest. "Funny you should ask that. Right at the moment, I mean."

"What do you mean?" Wardy flinched.

"Heinrich has been hinting about 'major commitments' lately. It's gotten me wondering: Is he trying to get out of the relationship—or, conversely, to get into the relationship more seriously?"

Wardy did not know how to say what his own opinion on the matter was, so he tried to remain blank, but he couldn't stop fidgeting.

His mother laughed. "You're acting like a frightened jackrabbit. Are you still holding out for a reunion between your father and me?"

"No—sorry. Go on."

"Well, I've thought it over, and I wonder if Heinrich is planning to ask me to go to Europe this summer—along with you to the Summer Youth Institute. What do you think of that?"

"Right now." Wardy tightened his grip on his mug. "Right now I'm not sure he even wants *me* to go to Europe. He was pretty frosted about my skipping out on the Sci-Tech Exposition."

Tapping her cup, his mother appeared to be thinking. "Hmmm. I thought I detected some serious animosity on his part tonight. More, perhaps, than a forgotten date might warrant." She glanced at Wardy and then went back to her tapping. "Do you think Heinrich's attentions to me might have something to do with his relationship with you?" Silence. Tap. Tap. Tap. When she focused on him again, her eyes held a long-forgotten, pleading expression that Wardy hadn't seen since he was a little kid, when she'd tried to talk him into going out for the band—or maybe it was the school play.

"It's very complex and confusing. Mr. Guterman and me . . .you . . .everything. He's done so much for me—probably changed my life forever, but I can't go along with everything he wants of me. He knows that, and he doesn't like it."

"What kinds of things? Is this just rebellion—the same kind of rebellion you've always seemed to have against me?" His mother furrowed her brow.

He thought about how he would answer her. "Rebellion—okay. If that's what you want to call it. Because a lot of times I've felt what you want for me isn't right. And I know what Mr. Guterman expects—total dedication to science at the expense of everything else—isn't right for me, either."

When his mother spoke, her voice was sad. "The same way I tried to force you into my plans for your life. Is that the way you see it?"

Blinking rapidly, his voice came out harsh. "I'm tired of everybody telling me what to do when I've got my own ideas. When I was so down—screwed up everything—I wanted you to support me. But, you thought of me as a failure. You wanted a 'red-blooded American kid.' " He made air quotes with his fingers. "Yes, I've felt pressures under Guterman, in a different way. Mr. Guterman—he's so sure of what he wants. And he's smart. He knows how to use people. He manipulates them, gets them to do his bidding—almost like a hypnotist. He's done that to both of us."

Thoughtfully, Gwen studied her son's face. "When did you get so smart?" she asked quietly. "When? All of a sudden, it's like you're the father and I'm the child—learning at your knee. You've known it all along, haven't you? That Heinrich Guterman was using me to gain more control over you? Haven't you?"

Wardy inclined his head slightly. "For a long time I've thought about it, I guess. But I've finally admitted it to myself. That's the way he operates, you know. Smart, like I said."

Unexpectedly, his mother put her hand on his shoulder. "It seems I've acted like a fool—a silly schoolgirl fool—about your teacher, about you . . .about a lot of things."

Wardy felt uncomfortable; he couldn't think what to say to her.

When she faced him again, there were tears in her eyes. "So many changes in our lives, Wardy. So much to cope with. I think it was too much stress for me when your father left. I wasn't strong enough to keep everything going—my job, Leslie, you and all your problems. When Heinrich came along—well, I didn't have the good sense to resist his charm." She wiped her eyes. "I'd like for us to try to work out some of these things—together. It's not too late for us to start over—do things right—is it? Is it?"

In his chest Wardy could feel the thud of doubt. Would she feel the same way tomorrow? Or would the familiar hostility come up with the sun? Still, he found himself responding almost involuntarily. "Okay, Mom. I'll try, if you will."

"I know we can't erase all the bad times or eliminate the scars. But we can talk. Communicate. Share."

Wardy winced. She sounded like a guest on a daytime TV talk show—earnest and determined, spilling her guts for the ratings.

No. Not fair. Give her a chance. It's all she's asking for. Just a chance.

"l guess so. I'm willing to give it a try."

"It'll be hard work, getting rid of the old, destructive habits. But I'm going to keep my word. I promise." She stood up. "Now, let's get some sleep. This has been quite a day. Let's see what morning brings."

Morning. I know what I'm going to do in the morning. Round two, Meg Reilly.

****

"Hello, Meg?" Wardy tried to speak quietly. "This is Wardy." There was silence on the other end, but he kept on. "Sorry to call you so early in the morning, but I *have* to talk to you—before school starts today." Wardy heard a sound that might have been a sigh, or maybe a sob, then a click. She had hung up on him. Well, he deserved it—he knew that. If only he'd had the strength of character to ignore Guterman's bidding. Would he ever convince Meg he'd changed? He tried again. "Meg, please. Please don't hang up! I know I've been a rat. I'm sorry. Really sorry. I…" He heard the distinct click that meant she'd hung up on him again. *Round two. Lost another one. But there's lots of fight left in me, Meg. The match isn't over yet. Not yet.*

Still deep in thought, Wardy decided to jog to school instead of taking the bus. He didn't feel like chattering at the bus stop and being crowded with all the other kids on the big, lumbering vehicle. Rounding the last turn into the school parking lot, he slowed down to catch his breath. Leaning against the bike rack, he inhaled and exhaled slowly, his mind still occupied with the problem of getting Meg to talk to him. He was convinced that if he could just get her ear, she'd understand—allow them to be friends again.

"Wardy." The whisper electrified him. He whipped around in astonishment. Hesitantly, Meg stepped from behind the red aluminum wall of the temporary building at the corner of the backstop. "I was waiting for your bus, but I'm glad you walked instead. I thought you might." Moving around the building, she faced him. "I'm sorry I hung up on you this morning. I thought about it afterwards—how you've been trying to talk to me. I decided I ought to listen."

"Meg! I thought I'd lost you for sure. I've been wrong. You figured Mr. Guterman out a long time ago, but I was too stubborn—too vain—to listen to you. I was so impressed by all the attention he was giving me...I'm sorry—you'll never know how sorry." Reaching out a hand, he touched her arm lightly, almost afraid that by touching her, he'd break the mirage and she'd be gone. "It's all over with Guterman. He'll never dominate me again."

"I'm glad, Wardy. Glad you've seen Mr. Guterman for what he is."

Students began to arrive for school. "Let's go sit on the steps of the temp building. Nobody will be there for a while, and we can talk without an audience." They moved toward the small structure tucked away from the central building. They dropped their books on the bottom step, then sat higher up, conversing in low tones. "Meg— I— I've missed you. I wish I'd never written you that note. I've regretted it a thousand times."

"Then we're almost even," she whispered. "I regretted getting it a thousand times, too. It meant you'd bought into Guterman's way—his plan."

"You know, the sad thing is that he did so much for me—changed me from an ugly duckling, made me feel worthwhile and intelligent and capable at a time when I was on a long downhill slide. He picked me up, stood me on my feet. Guterman showed me how to succeed."

"But, Wardy," Meg's soft voice broke in, "you've always had all those good qualities. And you know you can believe in yourself now. Stand on your own. You'll never lose that."

"It's hard to accept that he was trying to make me into something I'm not—bend me to his way of thinking about people, about what's valuable in life. Grandma Lou thinks he was even trying to further his own career—use me for that."

Meg gave a little shrug. "That doesn't surprise me. When you first told me he'd seen the laser, I wondered then if he'd try to twist your wonderful experiment—distort it into something for himself." She sounded bitter. "I learned enough about people like him at the SL Center."

"Too bad I didn't listen to you."

They watched the growing crowds milling around the parking lot and streaming into the main school building. "Guess we'd better go in," Meg said. "Anyway, my backside is frozen to this cold step, I think." For the first time, she smiled. Her cheeks glowed above her red scarf.

"Then we can be friends like we were before…? We can talk on the phone, stay after school together?" He was almost afraid to hear her answer.

Again, she smiled, this time a little wanly. "Yes. We can be friends again, but you're still going to be busy with tutorials after school, getting ready for the Summer

Youth Institute."

"No, no—that's all over. I've made up my mind. I'm going to see Guterman after school today, in fact, and tell him. My working relationship with him has been blown to bits like…like a can of beans." He gave a short laugh. "It won't work anymore."

"You're serious? You'd give up the chance to go to Germany this summer?"

Wardy nodded, his face lit up. "Can you believe something else has come up? Not a summer in Germany—but in California. Dr. Lowry—remember, the professor who wrote and helped me with Big Vi? He was at my house last night, and he wants me to write an article for a science journal. I may get a scholarship to the workshop in California at his college if they like it."

"Oh! That's wonderful."

"Dr. Lowry wants me to ask you to make the diagrams for the laser article. He says it's better if the work is done by students—it's a student-written magazine. There might also be a scholarship in it for you."

"You want me to draw your laser diagrams? Oh. Do you think . . .?"

"It's your special talent. It would make the article so much better—and give you a chance for a scholarship, too. How about it?"

They slid down the short steps to the ground. "Will you do it? We can work together after school—it'll be like old times."

On impulse, she thrust out her hand as though to shake on the deal. "Okay, I'm in."

He reached to take her hand. It was warm and soft, and the touch filled him with longing. She raised her eyes to his, and suddenly his arms were around her. Pressing her cheek against his chest, she breathed short, quick breaths. He could feel her heart beating through his open coat as he held her close. "Meg, Meg," he said against her hair. "I'm glad you're back."

Chapter Twenty

"So, there really was a skeleton in Guterman's closet." Wardy shook his head in disbelief. "And all along I refused to listen to the gossip about the 'Guterman scandal.' Who'd ever think!"

Meg wagged her head. "Wish I could say I told you so but it surprises even me."

"Tell me again—how did your father find out? I haven't got that straight yet. It's so unbelievable."

"Well, my dad teaches at Fordwell University, you know, and he heard about it from a professor in the physics department."

"You mean, Guterman was actually fired from the college in Germany because of...because he plagiarized something? Took somebody else's work and claimed it for his own? It just doesn't seem possible. He's so brilliant, so precise. Why? Why would he do such a thing?"

"Dad thinks it had something to do with the 'publish or perish' requirement for professors—they're under a lot of pressure to publish their findings. An ambitious man like Guterman—he probably figured it was a quick way to have it all."

They strolled through the park on the way to Wardy's house to work on their article for Dr. Lowry. Unseasonably warm, the air promised an early spring. Under a giant oak tree, they stopped. Wardy spread his jacket on the ground, and they both sat, lounging against the huge, gnarled roots.

Wardy picked up a smooth stone and examined it reflectively. "So, Guterman comes to America and tries to redeem himself by snagging a smart kid to take back to the Summer Youth Institute. Somebody he can claim as a protégé—me. Big Vi was the unexpected plum."

Meg laughed shortly. "Whew! It gives me goose bumps."

"How come Guterman didn't go to jail or get disbarred or whatever they do to bad teachers? Did your dad know anything about that?"

"Guterman denied it—said it was the other scientist who was at fault. And the evidence wasn't conclusive. But it didn't seem good for Guterman, so he finally agreed to leave the school if the charges were dropped. That's when he applied to be an exchange teacher. Somehow Guterman's past must have slipped through the cracks when he was hired to teach at Evanstown." Meg shrugged. "If they know now, they'll probably let him finish out the term anyway." She gave Wardy a sly glance. "By the way, the scientist who accused Guterman of plagiarism was a woman."

"No kidding." He whistled. "I'm beginning to see the whole picture a lot more clearly."

"Oh, and I heard something else you might be interested in." Meg covered her smile with her hand. "A bunch of guys were just suspended. Did you know that? Suspended for setting up a derogatory page on Facebook—a page linked to Evanstown High, even though they claimed they'd done it all outside of school."

"Huh?" Wardy was interested.

"The dummies called it the *Eaglebait* page. Duh!

The Evanstown Eagles' signature cheer? I guess it was hard to deny it was a school-based bullying tactic."

"Well, I never bothered to read those comments, anyway," Wardy responded. "Once I got involved with Big Vi and bio lab with you. . .well. . .the taunting didn't seem so important anymore, I guess."

For a while, they sat in companionable silence. Wardy knew what he wanted to say next, but he wasn't sure how to put it into words, even after all his practice. Sitting up straighter, he cleared his throat. "Hey, Meg, next Saturday's my birthday, you know? Mom's cooking me a special dinner—she said I could invite you...if you'd like to come. We could go out to a movie afterwards—what do you think?" *There, I've done it. Asked her for a date. Will she turn me down? Make me feel like a fool?* His heart pounded as he watched her face—listened and waited.

Her answer seemed to take a long time coming. She sat with lowered eyes, tracing a pattern in the dirt with her finger. Finally, she replied. "Gee, it—it sounds like fun. I mean, I feel honored—your birthday. But I don't know. . ." Her voice trailed off, and she dropped her gaze again.

Don't rush it. Don't push her. She's so sensitive, and our relationship's still delicate. Patience. Patience. He had one more card to play. He took a deep breath. "Grandma Lou's coming up from the beach house for my birthday. I'd sure like you to meet her—and her to meet you."

"Grandma Lou?" Meg's eyes showed her interest. "I feel like I already know her. Isn't that strange?"

"My grandmother's always liked you, Meg. When we were...having our problems, she told me I should hang on to you. She liked you, sight unseen."

Meg took a little breath. "I'll come for your birthday," she whispered. "I'd like that very much."

Wardy felt weak with relief. He was glad he was sitting down, but Meg seemed unaware of his nervous state. "How's your grandmother doing now that she's retired?" she asked.

"Oh," he said, his voice cracking a bit, "she's going on with her life and work just like she said she would. She says she's slowing down, but she's an amazing person. She continues to paint, just not traveling for exhibitions and stuff." He leaned against the big root again, feeling emotionally exhausted, but happy.

"Are you doing anything else special for your fifteenth birthday?"

"Oh, yeah. Dad called. He wants me to go to a big invitational track meet at Fordwell University. He says there'll be some Olympic stars there."

"You don't talk much about your father." Meg's voice was serious. The breeze blew her fine hair away from her face. Wardy realized anew how pretty she was—how much he wanted their friendship to be something more. Would he ever stand a chance at romance with Meg? She'd accepted his invitation, but he'd had to do some subtle arm-twisting. He forced his thoughts back to the conversation. "I...I just can't accept Dad's swinging-single lifestyle. I hate it, but I don't know how to tell him without making him mad." Wardy squirmed with discomfort. "Even my sister Leslie hates it. It's the one thing we agree on."

"But he invited you to go to the meet with him. That's good, isn't it?"

"Dad knows I like watching sports. He's the one

who got me hooked in the first place. I think he's trying to do something he knows I'll enjoy. Just the two of us. He made a point of telling me that. None of his cute young chicks tagging along this time. And Leslie's not invited."

Meg hesitated, took a breath, and responded. "I'm glad I got to know you this year," she said abruptly. "And I'd like to think we both learned something from the experience with Mr. Guterman—that it wasn't all bad." She got to her feet a little stiffly. "Don't you think we ought to get going? If we sit here much longer, we'll be out of the mood for our work for Dr. Lowry."

Getting to work was the last thing on Wardy's mind, but he knew he'd have to be satisfied with one victory at a time. He and Meg were friends again. They were going out together next weekend. The romance he hoped for would have to evolve slowly, naturally from there. *Don't force it. Let it be. Time will tell.*

Still talking about his upcoming birthday, they walked along the sidewalk that led out of the park. Abruptly, Meg stopped and pointed down. In faded red letters, now almost unreadable on the roughened concrete, were scrawled the words *Wardy Spinks Is Eaglebait.*

A word about the author...

A career educator, Susan Coryell is also a life-long writer. Previous publications by The Wild Rose Press include The Overhome Trilogy, a cozy mystery/Southern Gothic series and a murder mystery. In 2022, she independently published a children's picture book.

Winner of the NY Library's "Books for the Teen Age," and the International Reading Association's "Young Adult Choice," EAGLEBAIT is cited by a number of anti-bullying associations.

One of Susan's favorite activities is to talk with budding writers at schools, writers' conferences and workshops.

When not writing, the author enjoys boating, kayaking, yoga and pickle ball. She and her husband love to travel, especially to visit family in Hawaii.

http://www.susancoryellauthor.com

Thank you for purchasing
this publication of The Wild Rose Press, Inc.

For questions or more information
contact us at
info@thewildrosepress.com.

The Wild Rose Press, Inc.
www.thewildrosepress.com